"Something clearly exists bet[ween us], Roth. Something that gives me so much peace it scares me."

He hummed a sound that could have been interpreted as understanding or confusion, then his arms tightened around her a hint more. Was that his way of saying he felt the same way? She needed him to use words.

"Why are you afraid of me, Roth?" That was the only logical explanation. The only thing that made sense.

Roth chuckled, the smooth, sexy sound caressing her ears.

He placed a finger under her chin and tilted her head up. "Woman, do you really think I'm afraid of you?"

There was no need to be, but she replied, "Yes."

"I'm not afraid, Tressa. Just cautious."

"Am I a risk?"

"Yes," he said without blinking.

Now they were getting somewhere. "Am I one worth taking?" She could tell by the way he studied her that the question had caught him off guard. Bringing her mouth within inches of his, she teased him in the same way he'd teased [her ?]

His j[aw ?] I think
you a[

Dear Reader,

Thank you so much for purchasing *Soaring on Love*! Whether you're trying one of my novels for the very first time or are already a #joyaveryromance reader, your support is everything. I appreciate each and every one of you!

Because of his past, Roth would consider himself a hard man to love. It's a darn good thing Tressa doesn't see it this way. Nothing can break down barriers quicker than love. Just wait and see…

I hope you enjoy Tressa and Roth's love story just as much as I enjoyed writing it.

Until next time, HAPPY READING!

Love and light,

Joy

By the way: I love interacting with readers, so let's connect:

www.JoyAvery.com

www.Facebook.com/AuthorJoyAvery

www.Twitter.com/AuthorJoyAvery

www.Instagram.com/AuthorJoyAvery

authorjoyavery@gmail.com

Soaring on Love

JOY AVERY

H HARLEQUIN® KIMANI™ ROMANCE

Recycling programs
for this product may
not exist in your area.

ISBN-13: 978-1-335-21653-3

Soaring on Love

Copyright © 2018 by Joy Avery

For questions and comments about the quality of this book please contact us
at CustomerService@Harlequin.com.

Printed in U.S.A.

Joy Avery works as a customer service assistant. By night, the North Carolina native travels to imaginary worlds—creating characters whose romantic journeys invariably end happily ever after.

Since she was a young girl growing up in Garner, Joy knew she wanted to write. Stumbling onto romance novels, she discovered her passion for love stories; instantly, she knew these were the type of stories she wanted to pen.

Joy is married with one child. When not writing, she enjoys reading, cake decorating, pretending to expertly play the piano, driving her husband insane and playing with her two dogs.

Books by Joy Avery

Harlequin Kimani Romance

In the Market for Love
Soaring on Love

Dedicated to the dream.

Acknowledgments

To everyone who made this book possible…
THANK YOU!

To everyone who has supported me
on this glorious journey…
THANK YOU!

To my readers…
THANK YOU! THANK YOU! THANK YOU!

A special THANK YOU to my Joyrider Street Team.
You ladies are priceless!

A special, special THANK YOU to my editor
Shannon Criss! You made this possible.
I will forever be grateful!

Chapter 1

Roth Lexington leaned against the banister of the upper-level balcony inside The Underground Jazz House—The Underground, for short—nursing a glass of bourbon. The amber liquid had always been his drink of choice, ever since he'd taken his first sip at thirteen. "It'll make you a man," he'd been told. He was definitely a man, but he wasn't sure the bourbon had anything to do with it.

Taking a swig, he savored the earthy notes. A fire flared in his chest, but it wasn't from the whiskey. This inferno ignited from envy. With a tight jaw, he observed the partygoers below. He soaked in their laughs, their smiles, their congratulatory hugs and handshakes for the future bride and groom.

Normally, nothing soothed him like a smooth beverage and the silky sounds of jazz, but neither did much for him now. And he knew why. The reason stood several feet below him in the form of the sexiest woman in the room. Also, the guest of honor at this engagement party he'd reluctantly attended.

Tressa Washington.

Since the first time he'd laid eyes on the ravishing ER nurse several months ago in his best friend's living room, she'd danced in his thoughts. Danced sensual moves. Provocative moves. Seductive moves. Moves that had forced him awake in a hot sweat on several occasions. In his thirty-six years, he couldn't recall a woman ever having this kind of effect on him.

He didn't like it. He didn't like it at all.

Stunning in a fitted off-white jumpsuit, Tressa stood out among the sixty or so people in attendance. Tiny curls framed her round face, lightly touched with makeup. Though she didn't need any makeup at all, really. That was how stunning she was.

Engulfed in conversation with a group of women, her lips—the ones he craved to leave kiss swelled and aching—curled into a smile, and those dimples he'd grown to adore pierced her chocolate-brown cheeks. His gaze burned a heated path along her voluptuous body, stopping briefly to appreciate her ample breasts. They'd fit in his grasp perfectly.

It took a real man to handle dangerous curves like hers. And as he'd stated before, he was a man.

A knot tightened in his stomach. How he'd love to suckle nipples he'd teased with his thumbs to tautness. He curtailed his thoughts when he felt a tightening in his boxers. Wearing a hard-on for the bride-to-be in the middle of her engagement party would be a shit thing to do. But dammit, he couldn't help that Tressa turned him all the way on. He wanted her so badly he ached. Forbidden fruit was always so damn tempting.

Loud laughter drew his attention to Tressa's fiancé. *Cyrus Williams*. Even the thought of the man's name put a sour taste in his mouth. A cornball name for a cornball. Damn he hated that man. Or more accurately, envied him. Cyrus had something he wanted—Tressa's warm body pressed up against his.

Pushing his envy aside, Roth still got a bad vibe from this Cyrus character. He'd always been good at reading people and something about Tressa's soon-to-be husband screamed *shady*. Roth blew out a heavy breath. But Cyrus was none of his business, and neither was Tressa. And if he told himself that a few more hundred times, maybe he'd actually be convinced. He slid his eyes back to her.

As if sensing his ogling, Tressa shifted in his direction. The instant their gazes locked, a lightning bolt of desire seared through him. She smiled at him in that warm, welcoming manner he'd become accustomed to. A smile like that wasn't easily forgotten. But that was exactly what he needed to do. Forget. Forget that soul-stirring gesture and the woman donning it.

Tressa's best friend, Vivian—his best friend Alonso's wife—said something that drew Tressa's attention. Tressa slid her gaze away, allowing him to breathe again. Maybe he was being absurd, but he'd got the feeling she'd regretted ending their connection just as much as he had. Yeah, absurd.

Alonso clapped him on the shoulder. "Careful. The way you're staring at the bride could give someone the wrong idea. Namely, her soon-to-be husband." He laughed.

She wasn't a bride yet.

Roth and Alonso had been friends since way back. Over the years, Alonso had kept him out of so much trouble and got him into his fair share, as well. He didn't trust many people, but he trusted Alonso with his life.

Roth continued, still coveting something he'd never have, "You know if this was back in the day, she'd be mine, right?"

Yes, it was a cocky statement but also a true one. When he was young and dumb, he would not have hesitated to pursue Tressa at full throttle, regardless of her *situation*. Luckily for Cyrus, he'd become a far better man than he'd once been.

Alonso chuckled. "Trust me, I know. I'm surprised you came. You sounded a little iffy when we talked earlier."

Roth pulled his attention away from Tressa before he overheated. Taking another swig from his glass, he paused for a moment to savor the rich flavors. "Figured I'd swing by on my way out of town."

"Out of town?"

"Headed to my place in the mountains."

Alonso quirked a brow. "Alone?"

"That's a good question." Powerless against it, he sought out Tressa again. When their gazes locked, electricity—raw and powerful—slammed through him, causing a puff of air to escape. *What in the hell was that?* Alarm triggered his defenses, sending flares up like Fourth of July fireworks. He needed rescuing.

"You all right, man?" Alonso asked.

No, he wasn't. He wouldn't be all right until he'd got Tressa out of his system.

* * *

As one of the women went on and on about something, Tressa slid an inconspicuous glance to her watch—a flashy piece packed with diamonds—that Cyrus had given her as an engagement gift. He was good at giving expensive gifts. She just wished he were as generous with his time. In the past two weeks, they'd barely seen one another. As an investment banker, he should understand the importance of investing in the future, as well as in the right commodities.

She gave an occasional nod and displaced smile, just to present the illusion of listening. *Will this party ever end?* It'd only been an hour since her family and friends had all gathered to celebrate what should have been one of the most exciting nights of her life.

It wasn't.

There were a number of reasons she could have rattled off as to why, but the most severe one hovered above like a sexy gargoyle watching over the city.

Roth Lexington.

Simply thinking his name made her insides flutter. Then she scolded her body for the defiant act. Plenty of times she warned her system against responding to Roth. And plenty of times it'd disobeyed her.

Don't look at him. I repeat, do not look at him.

As if her body would choose today of all days to start listening to her. *Defiant.* Her brain sent her gaze to the balcony. The man was as tempting as the glowing hot-doughnut sign at Krispy Kreme. Who in the hell could resist? Definitely not her. But in this case, she had to. She was getting married.

Roth stood chatting with his best friend, Alonso. The mere sight of him pounded her insides like a sensual jackhammer against stubborn concrete. From any angle, he was gorgeous. Tall, a few inches over six feet, a body that would be the envy of any athletic trainer, skin the tone of the best imported cocoa beans and a gleaming smile that rivaled the sun. *That damn smile.* In a quiet setting, it could hypnotize a woman into doing reckless things. Trust her, she knew.

When Roth's attention slid to her, she gasped from the shock of awareness that scorched her soul. He flashed a half smile. She returned the gesture, then yanked her focus away from him before she melted into a puddle of lust in the middle of her own engagement party.

Damn. Why did that man cloud her better judgment and distort her common sense? *Stop it, Tressa! You're getting married in one month. February 18*, she reminded herself. But looking was okay, right? As long as she didn't touch. She gnawed at the corner of her lip. But she had touched. Oh, God, how she wanted to touch again.

She'd never been the unfaithful type, but when Roth had pulled her into his arms and kissed her senseless, she hadn't done a damn thing to break free. A reel of the kiss in her best friend's kitchen played in her head. Recalling how good his mouth had felt pressed against hers caused her lips to tingle. She touched two fingers to them.

It'd been the best damn kiss she'd ever experienced in her life. They'd both agreed that what had happened had been a huge mistake and had vowed to never mention it again. But a kiss like that haunted you. It wasn't something easily purged from your system. But, Lord, had she tried to purge it, along with this ornate desire to... *To what?* What did she really want from Roth?

Everything, she ruefully admitted. So why in the hell was she about to marry another man? *Because Cyrus is the right choice.* She eyed the gaudy diamond on her finger. So why didn't she feel the same exhilaration when she looked at Cyrus as she did when she eyed Roth? *It'll come*, she told herself. *Give it time.*

The air in the room grew thick, and she struggled to breathe. Was she having a panic attack? Fresh air. She needed fresh air. Weaving her way through the crowd, she escaped unseen through a side door. On the massive stone patio, she sucked in a few deep breaths. After several minutes her pounding heart returned to its normal steady beat. But she still felt as if she were plummeting.

The chill of the winter night air jarred her, making her regret not grabbing a jacket. She cradled herself in her arms to generate some heat. Closing her eyes, she appreciated the stillness of the night. But even the tranquil setting couldn't silence her thoughts and they popped right back open, the world rushing in.

Fools rush in.

She wasn't sure why the phrase blared at full volume in her thoughts. *Fools rush in.* Was she rushing into this? At thirty-four, shouldn't she be married? Some of her friends were already married with several kids. Her mother's voice played in her head and she smiled. *If your friends jumped off a roof, would you jump, too?*

No, Mommy, but... She sighed. Her biological clock was tick, tick, ticking away. She wanted kids. A houseful of germy, whiny, adorable, lovable kids. She thought about Jamison and her eyes burned with impending tears. Pushing thoughts of the boy away, she refocused.

Cyrus is a good man. An honorable man. A respectable man. So why did it feel like she was about to make the biggest mistake of her life?

Tilting her head heavenward, she whispered, "God, please give me a sign."

"Escaping your own party?" The voice came from behind.

Tressa flinched. *That was fast.* Ignoring Roth as the sign—for now—she turned toward him. No man should have been allowed to look that damn good in a simple black suit. On any other man, it would have been forgettable apparel. Something told her this image would linger in her thoughts all night.

Finding her words, she said, "Um…no. Not escaping. I just needed some fresh air. So many people inside. It's a bit stuffy. How'd you know I was out here?"

Roth leaned against the banister, crossing his legs at the ankle. "Instinct, I guess."

Instinct, her ass. She'd felt the caress of his eyes on her all night. She may have escaped everyone else, but she hadn't escaped his watchful eye. "And here I am, believing I'd made a clean getaway."

"Getaway, huh? What—or who—are you running from?"

Curious eyes probed her. "No one."

"Hmm."

Why did that *hmm* sound so accusing? Roth straightened to his full height. They stood in silence for a moment, simply staring at one another. The intensity in his eyes made her knees wobble, but she refused to turn away. If he wanted to assert dominance, he'd have to find a less willful opponent.

Then he folded his arms across his chest and the

move rattled her, because his biceps blossomed into cannonballs and strained against the tailored suit coat— it fit him far too well to be off-the-rack.

"So, fresh air is the only reason you're out here?" he said.

Regrouping, Tressa said, "What other reason would there be?"

He shrugged one wide shoulder. "I don't know. It looked like you were having some kind of anxiety attack. I came out to check on you."

Tressa released a nervous laugh. "What? No. An anxiety attack?" She brushed his accurate words off. "No." How was he diagnosing her with anything? He was an aerospace engineer, not a doctor. But the fact that he was concerned about her warmed her insides. "I'm fine. Like I said, it was stuffy in there. I came out—"

"For fresh air," he said, completing her sentence.

"Yeah." A corner of his mouth lifted into a sexy smile and she chastised herself for staring so hard at his lips. Lifting her eyes to his, she mumbled, "I'm just fine."

"Good. You're going to catch your death out here, Nurse Washington." Roth removed his suit coat and draped it over her shoulders. "Better?"

Lost in his manly scent, she mumbled, "You smell fantastic." Immediately realizing she'd actually said the words out loud, her cheeks burned with awkwardness. "Um, yes. Better. Thank you. W-what about you? Now you're going to catch your death or at least pneumonia." She'd been around Roth plenty. Why now was she turning into a bumbling fool?

"I don't get sick," he said.

Roth slid his hands into his pockets. The move

caused his biceps to flex again, and she imagined wrapping her hands around them as he made slow, sweet love to her. "I see. You muscle—muscle—*must*," she spit out. "You must have a strong immune system." *Bumbling fool.*

"I guess so. You and your fiancé seem happy together."

The odd timing of his words took her by surprise. "Thank you." She shifted away from him before he saw the uncertainty in her eyes and stared out into the darkness. Were she and Cyrus a doting couple? Was that what people saw when they looked at them—happiness?

Roth leaned in slightly. "Are you happy?"

Alarmed by the question, Tressa snapped, "Yes. Why would you ask that?" Then she regretted the sharp bite in her tone.

Roth pulled one hand from his pocket and flashed a palm. "I didn't mean to upset you. It's just…" He shrugged. "It's just that most women seem over the moon when they're about to walk down the aisle."

Was he suggesting she wasn't over the moon? She was plenty over the damn moon. "Yeah, well, I'm not most women."

"Oh, I definitely know this."

A glint of something flashed in his demanding brown eyes and it smoothed her ruffled feathers. Again, their gazes held for a long, quiet, intense moment. Were these probing glances power plays between them, or was it that when they looked at each other, they simply became lost in each other's souls? There was something soothing about the way Roth looked at her, a look that could polish rough edges.

"Well, I'll let you get back to your fresh air. Congratulations again on your engagement. Good night."

Tressa's brow furrowed. "Wait." The word came too urgently. "You're not leaving, are you? The party, I mean." Why did the possibility bother her so much?

"Shortly. I promised two of your aunts dances, and I don't make promises I can't keep. Then I need to get on the road before it gets too late."

Yeah, her aunts—and several other of her female family members—had grown quite fond of Roth. Alonso, too. But Vivian had intervened on that one, crushing all of their dreams about her man. "On the road?"

"I have a cabin in Silver Point. The mountains," he clarified. "About four hours away."

"Huh."

"Don't look so surprised."

"It's not that. I just took you for more of a city dweller."

"I love being in the mountains. No one near for miles. Absolute peace and quiet. I can go on my deck and play my sax as early or as late as I want without disturbing a soul." His brow furrowed. "That reminds me. I don't think I locked my vehicle." Obviously, he noticed Tressa's where-did-that-come-from expression. "Juliette's in there—my saxophone."

"You call your saxophone Juliette?"

"Yes."

"Okay." Tressa recalled the first and last time she'd watched him play his sax. It was the most alluring thing she'd ever witnessed. He'd made absolute love to the instrument. The way he'd held it, caressed it, wrapped his lips around it… Her cheeks heated just thinking about him playing her like a saxophone.

What is wrong with you? You are about to be a married woman. Her mother would be so disappointed in her for lusting over one man while engaged to another. She massaged the side of her neck. "So, the mountains?"

Roth continued, "Mountain air is great for clearing the mind and rejuvenating the soul."

Sounded like her kind of place. "You sound like a travel brochure. I've never been to the mountains." The declaration sounded as if she was trolling for an invite. She kicked herself.

"Really?"

She nodded.

"Well, anytime you and your husband want to get away, let me know. You're more than welcome to use my place. It's not much, but it's cozy and intimate. The perfect escape for a couple in love."

A couple in love. Boy, he was laying it on thick. Tressa returned her attention to the darkness.

"Tressa, are you sure—"

Whipping toward him, she said, "Yes, I'm sure I want to marry Cyrus. Why does everyone keep asking me that?"

"I…was actually going to ask you if you were sure standing in this cold was a good idea."

She eyed Roth dumbly, her level of embarrassment soaring to unprecedented heights. "Oh." Compassion danced in Roth's eyes as he scrutinized her. No doubt he saw right through her. How was that possible?

Standing dangerously close to her, he said, "If you ever need someone to talk to, I'm a great listener."

"Thank you, but I'm—"

"Fine," he said, completing her sentence for the second time tonight.

"You're getting pretty good at finishing my thoughts."

The corner of his mouth lifted into a sexy smirk. "If I thought that had been a compliment, I would say thank you."

He was getting pretty good at reading her, too, because it had been a cynical remark. When she attempted to remove his coat to return it, he stopped her.

"Just leave it with the hostess when you're done. She'll make sure I get it. Good night, Tressa. Enjoy the rest of your party."

"Enjoy the mountains."

When Roth disappeared through the doors, she tightened his coat around her, inhaling his delicious scent. Had Roth's intrusion really been her sign? She laughed at herself. No. Tilting her head again, she said, "God, if you send me a sign, please make it a pronounced one. I don't want to miss it."

Twenty minutes later Tressa found herself on the dance floor with her soon-to-be husband. With her thoughts still stuck on her encounter with Roth, she barely processed Cyrus's presence.

"Should it bother me that my fiancée smells like another man's cologne?"

This snagged her attention. Reeling back, she stared into Cyrus's probing green eyes. "Excuse me?"

"You smell like *him*."

Playing coy, she said, "*Him*, who?"

Cyrus's features hardened and deep lines etched into his caramel-toned forehead. "You know what *him* I'm referring to. Don't try to play me for a fool." His expression softened. "I love you, Tressa. I want to spend the rest of my life with you. But I need to know."

She searched his sad eyes. "Need to know what, Cyrus?"

"I need to know... I need to know if you're sleeping with him."

Tressa froze, stunned by Cyrus's question. Her lips parted, but nothing readily escaped. Why in the world had Cyrus asked her that?

"I see the way he looks at you. Hell, he's been staring at you all night. Every damn move you make. I don't want to lose you. I don't want to lose you to him."

Cyrus's words broke her heart. At that moment she realized how unfair she'd been to him. Cradling his smooth face between her hands, she said, "I would never hurt you like that, Cyrus. You're the man I'm marrying, remember?"

A smile curled his lips and he eased his forehead against hers. "I love you, baby. I love you so much." His expression turned somber and he rested his hands on either side of her neck. "I've made mistakes, Tressa. But I swear I'm going to be a good husband to you."

Mistakes. What mistakes had he been referring to? Before she got the opportunity to ask, clapping sounded behind Cyrus. Tressa glanced over his shoulder, her gaze landing on a brown-skinned woman in a very revealing black gown. She wore a black fishnet veil that made her look as if she was in mourning.

"That was so beautiful," the woman said, nearing them. "Too bad it's nothing but a bunch of bull—"

"Natalie!" Cyrus barked. His nostrils flared and a vein pulsed in his neck. "What in the hell are you doing here?" he said through clenched teeth.

Fine lines etched into Tressa's forehead. "*Natalie?* You know this woman, Cyrus?"

"Yes, he does. *Very* well." Natalie placed her hands on her hips. "We had an *intimate* work relationship until a few days ago," she said with a smirk.

Cyrus looked as if he could snatch the woman's heart out with his hand. Spittle flew from his mouth when he said, "Shut the hell up, Natalie," through teeth gritted so tightly they should have all been ground to dust.

Whispers and words revealing shock among the small crowd now circling them, swirled around her. Tuning it all out, she zeroed in on Cyrus. "You should probably start talking right now. What's going on?"

"Yes, Cyrus. We'd both like to know what the hell is going on," Natalie added.

This time ignoring their party crasher, Cyrus turned to her. "Tressa. I made a mistake. We can—"

When he reached for her, she backed away. This was the mistake he referenced earlier. "How long?"

When he didn't answer, Natalie did. "Four months."

"Four—" The air seized in her lungs.

"Baby—"

Tears stung her eyes, but they were more angry than sentimental ones. "You lying, cheating, no-good, trifling bastard." She wrenched the ring from her finger and tossed it at him. Eyeing Natalie, she said, "He's all yours. The wedding is off."

Cyrus grabbed her arm. "No, you don't mean that."

A second later Tony—her three-hundred-pound ex-lineman cousin—clapped a large hand on Cyrus's shoulder. The look in his eyes suggested Cyrus release her now.

Obviously, Cyrus got the silent message, because his grip on her arm loosened, then fell away.

Several family members—including her visibly livid mother—swarmed around Cyrus like bees on the attack. They stung him with their not-so-gentle words of disapproval. As the room erupted in utter chaos, Tressa made her escape. She'd asked for a sign and, boy, had she got it.

Chapter 2

Amid all of the chaos, Roth eyed Tressa weaving her way through the room and toward the exit. She brushed past the outstretched hands of individuals undoubtedly offering their comfort and support. He tore down the stairs after her, but by the time he made it outside, she was nowhere in sight. Where in the hell had she vanished to so damn suddenly?

He squinted against the dark for any sign of movement. Nothing.

When the door banged open behind him and Cyrus's snake ass slithered out, dragging his hideous mistress behind him, Roth's jaw tightened in disgust.

Cyrus slid a razor-sharp glance in Roth's direction. Roth readied himself for a confrontation, but Cyrus only flashed a scornful expression, then escaped in the opposite direction.

After hanging around another half hour or so—just to see if Tressa resurfaced—he decided to head out, leaving instructions for Alonso to call him the minute he heard anything. Yanking open the door of his SUV, Roth slid behind the wheel and slumped in the seat. A part of him wanted to start the engine and follow through with his plans to leave, while another part of him—a much greater portion—wanted to hang back to make sure Tressa was okay.

He abandoned the idea of staying. Tressa definitely didn't need him to further complicate her life. Given what she'd just gone through, he was certain he was the last person she wanted to see. Not because he'd been in any way responsible for the debacle that had taken place, but because he was a man. And at this point she more than likely hated the entire male species.

And who could blame her? He'd certainly held a discord for the female population when he'd got his heart broken several years ago. Then he'd met Tressa a few months back and feelings he'd long abandoned rushed him like water released from a dam.

Four months.

Roth shook his head. That slimy bastard had cheated on Tressa almost their entire relationship. Via Alonso, he'd learned Tressa and that clown Cyrus had only dated a short time before they'd become engaged. Why even propose if he knew he had no intentions of being faithful?

Why would any man in his right mind sacrifice a woman like Tressa?

Roth recalled the expression on Tressa's face as she darted from the room. A mix of confusion and pain danced in her usually sparkling eyes. At that moment he really wanted to hurt Cyrus, if for nothing more than dimming her glow.

"Are we leaving?"

Roth jolted, then whipped around to see Tressa stretched across his back seat. *What the...* How in the hell had he missed seeing her when he'd got in? *Preoccupied*, he told himself. *Damn.* She'd nearly given him a heart attack.

Activating the interior lights, he scanned her body as if looking for any damage. When he saw her red, puffy eyes, he fought the urge to climb over the center console and pull her into his comforting arms. And though she had every right to cry, he wanted to advise her not to waste her tears on a lowlife like Cyrus.

Roth's words were gentle when he spoke. "Everyone is looking for you."

She hugged her arms around her body. "I don't want to be found. I can't handle the looks and whispers right now."

Being the voice of reason, he said, "People are worried about you, Tressa. They just want to know that you're all right. You really should—"

"Roth, please. Spare me the lecture. I don't have my car here. I need to go. Can you just get me away from here? Just drive. Please." Her voice was low, but screamed of exhaustion.

Tressa's sad, pleading eyes tugged at his heart. Who could blame her for wanting to avoid being poked and prodded like a lab rat by people's stares of pity? Facing forward, he cranked the engine, popped the gearshift into Drive and pulled away.

Silence filled the car for the first few minutes. Roth avoided plying her with the usual pacifiers: it's going to be okay, the pain will go away, look on the bright side. Instead, he stayed quiet because no words could ease the sting of betrayal. Only time could do that.

Roth adjusted the rearview mirror so that it settled on Tressa's face. He hated seeing her this way, a sad replica of her customarily jovial self. "Maybe we should call Vivian to let her know you're okay. She was really worried about you."

Tressa's eyes landed on his. Even through the reflection, their connection rang intense. Everything and nothing had changed. Though she'd ended her engagement, she was still off-limits. Maybe even more so now.

"I will," was all she said before sliding her gaze away.

"Should I take you home?"

"No. He'll probably be at my place. I don't want to see him. Ever."

Roth washed a hand over his mouth as if he was ironing his goatee. All he wanted to do was make her smile—laugh even. But he doubted anything he could have said or done would have accomplished that.

"Were you going to the mountains alone?"

An hour ago the answer would have been yes. But once he'd walked away from her on the balcony, he'd discovered a need for something—or in this case, someone—to take his mind off her. Still, he responded, "Yes, I'm going alone."

"You don't have a very good poker face."

Damn. She'd read him. Now he felt like a complete ass. All she needed was another man lying to her. "Why?"

"I guess because you don't lie enough to pull it off."

He chuckled. She was right. Since lying was what

people had done to him most of his life, he valued the truth more than most. But that wasn't the *why* he meant. "Not that. Why did you ask if I was going alone?"

Her gaze fixed on his again. She didn't need to answer for him to know she wanted an invite to his cabin. If her goal was to hide from the world, it would be the perfect escape for her. No one would find her in Silver Point. An hour ago the idea of him and Tressa *running off* together would have been damn appealing, but now it reeked of trouble. "Maybe you'd prefer a hotel? You wouldn't—"

"You don't want to be saddled with a jilted ex-bride-to-be. I get it."

Damn. Why did she have to make it sound so morbid? "That's not it, Tr—"

"Just drop me off at the nearest hotel. I've dealt with scarier things. I'll be fine."

Scarier things? What scarier things had she dealt with?

Ten minutes later they pulled up in front of the De Lore Hotel in downtown Raleigh. The sprawling building was the epitome of luxury. He'd heard nothing but great things about it. It even looked fancy. Concierge, bellmen, greeters. Tressa would be comfortable here. Much more comfortable than at his cramped cabin.

Why in the hell did he sound like he was trying to convince himself? And why did the idea of leaving her here alone bother him so damn much? It wasn't like he was abandoning her. She would be okay, right?

Once she was checked in, he'd call Vivian to come and comfort her. Her best friend was who she needed, not the man who constantly fantasized about making love to her. Roth brushed a hand over his close-cut hair.

A young man who'd been standing at what looked

like a podium and dressed in a black overcoat and gloves approached his SUV. When Roth lowered the window a gust of cold air rushed in. He welcomed the brisk breeze because it felt as if his system was over-heating.

"Good evening, sir. Welcome to the De Lore Hotel. Will you be staying with us this evening?"

"Ah…" *Shit. Spit it out, Lex. Say yes, she will. Say it.* His gaze slid to Tressa. When she rested her hand on the door handle to open it, his heart raced. *Don't do it, man. Don't do it.* "Actually, no. Maybe another time. Thank you." The window rose and he pulled off, leaving the man standing there.

Roth swiped his thumb back and forth against the steering wheel. *What in the hell are you doing? This woman of all women should not be in your back seat. And taking her to the cabin? The cabin's your sanctuary.*

A significant thought occurred to him. *What about the nightmares?* His past had a way of haunting him in his dreams. All he needed was to wake up scream-ing at the top of his lungs. It would scare the hell out of Tressa and embarrass the hell out of him. An occur-rence like that would break two of his cardinal rules: never show vulnerability and always maintain control. He'd learned a long time ago that being vulnerable got you hurt and losing control made you rash.

Her being at the cabin with him *period* would break the third: always wake up alone.

Two days. He could handle two days cooped up with the woman he'd dreamed about, fantasized about since the first day they met. *Two days.* No problem. Hell, it wasn't like he could actually make a move now anyway.

That would be a shit thing to do. She was vulnerable, grieving and probably out for a little sexual revenge.

The last point gave him pause. *Sexual revenge.* A woman scorned was capable of anything, right? Well, he'd never played the role of the rebound guy, and he wouldn't start now. Not even for Tressa. That alone should keep his libido in check.

"Thank you, Roth. I promise I won't get in your way."

He met Tressa's tender gaze through the rearview mirror and his heartbeat kicked up just a notch. *Oh, you're already getting in my way.* Influencing him to make bad decisions, testing his resolve, reminding him how it felt to crave something unattainable. "You'll like Silver Point," was all he said.

Roth swiped his thumb back and forth across the steering wheel, lost in his thoughts. This was the stupidest thing he'd done in a long while. Reckless, even. He couldn't be alone with Tressa. Yes, he had self-control, plenty of self-control. But this would require a whole lot of self-discipline.

His eyes slid to Tressa, who'd been watching him through the mirror. For a split second, he didn't regret pulling away from the hotel. Her eyes slid away, and after a short time, his did, too.

Four hours later they arrived at the cabin on the hill, as the townsfolk often called it. He popped the SUV into Park, then glanced back at Tressa. She'd fallen asleep two hours into the drive—or had pretended to be to avoid having to talk.

His insides did a shimmy watching her. She really was asleep now, because in the stillness, he could hear her soft snores. As far as bad decisions went, bringing Tressa here was the Grandfather Mountain of poor judgment calls. He just hoped it wouldn't backfire in his face.

Tressa assumed Roth's gentle touch was only in her dreams until his voice penetrated her slumber, and she realized he was trying to wake her. She cracked her eyes and squinted to focus. His handsome face slowly materialized. "How long have I been asleep?" she asked in a groggy voice.

"A couple of hours. Come on, Sleeping Beauty."

She took Roth's outstretched hand, the spark giving her the jolt of energy she needed. Gravel crunched under her feet as she stepped out of the vehicle. One of the first things she noticed—excluding the bone-chilling cold—was the quiet. No horns. No traffic. No bustling.

Yeah, this was the perfect place to rejuvenate her soul. Being here would be good for her. It would give her the time she needed to think and clear her cluttered thoughts. Inhaling a deep breath, she blew it out slowly. Already she felt…free.

The only light radiated from the full moon. She tilted her head and scrutinized a sky so clear it could have been a flawless oil painting. And the stars… Had she ever seen them twinkle more brightly?

And then there were the oversize trees. She performed a slow turn. Trees, trees and more trees surrounded them. Roth hadn't exaggerated about the privacy of this location. Not a single soul would be able to hear them scream if they were attacked.

The quaint cabin caught her eye. What it lacked in size, it made up for in charm. Built completely of logs, seven steps led to a nicely sized wraparound porch. A cobblestone chimney protruded from the roof. Several hours ago she would have tingled at the idea of her and Roth cuddled intimately in front of a wood-burning fireplace. Not now.

Roth startled her when he draped his coat over her shoulders. He'd obviously changed out of his suit at The Underground because now he wore a thick black sweater, jeans and a pair of black mountain boots. Despite her current state of mind, she could still appreciate how devastatingly attractive he was. "Thank you. I'm freezing." She shivered for effect.

"We can go into town in the morning and grab you some clothes. I'm sure you don't want to wear this the entire weekend." He fingered the thin fabric of her jumpsuit. "Regardless of how beautiful you look in it."

Disappointment flashed on Roth's face that suggested he regretted saying the words. Regardless, the compliment brought a lazy smile to her face. "It's gorgeous. Your cabin. Thank you again for bringing me here with you. I won't get in the way."

What she really wanted to say—ask actually—was why had he seemed so reluctant to bring her here at first, and what had changed his mind? But she decided against it. She was just happy she wouldn't have to be alone.

"Thanks. Like I said, it's not much, but I love it."

Tressa opened and closed her mouth several times.

"Ears popping?" Roth said.

"Yes."

"It's the altitude. You'll get used to it."

Moving to the back of the vehicle, Roth removed a bag and a large black case she assumed was his saxophone—Juliette—before they made their way inside, out of the cold. Or so she'd thought. It was as cold inside the cabin as it had been outside. Possibly a degree or two colder. She pulled the wool coat tighter around her shoulders.

"I believe it's warmer outside."

"I'll build a fire," Roth said. "It shouldn't take it long to warm up in here."

The interior wasn't at all what Tressa had expected. A mocha-colored leather sofa and a matching chair sat in the living area. Several pictures of airplanes hung throughout the room. A flat-screen television was mounted on the wall above the fireplace. A bookcase packed with books sat in one corner. Was it for decoration, or did Roth enjoy reading?

Her eyes trailed to the kitchen outfitted with all stainless steel appliances. A small dining area seamlessly melted the space together. A set of stairs led to what she assumed were the bedrooms. This was nice. Really nice.

The sound of the fire crackling curled Tressa's lips. It took her back to when she was a child and winters spent at her grandparents' house. Good times. Roth's voice faded Tressa's memories.

"Unfortunately, there's only one bed, but it's yours. I'll camp out on the sofa." He patted the plush-looking piece. "We're highly acquainted. I've fallen asleep in her warm arms many nights."

"No, Roth. I can't let you do that. I'll take the sofa. No argument," she said when protest danced in Roth's mesmerizing eyes. "Truly, it's fine." No way would she inconvenience him after he'd been so kind as to bring her here.

After a few seconds of scrutiny Roth shrugged. "Okay, but you're going to hate me in the morning."

As if that was possible. The perplexed look he gave her rattled her a bit. What was he attempting to decipher? How she was holding up? Why she'd wanted to come here with him? Would she be okay? She didn't know the answer to any of it.

To end his exhausting scrutiny, she said, "Please tell me you have food in this place. I'm starving."

"Yes, we do. I have someone who looks in on the place for me. When I let her know I'm coming, she always stocks the fridge."

She?

Jealousy was the last emotion Tressa expected, but a hint of it crept in. Could this have been the mystery woman he'd intended to spend the weekend with before she'd come along and derailed his plans? Was it selfish that she didn't regret spoiling his rendezvous? Yes.

"Well, let's just see what *she* brought, shall we?" If nothing else could, cooking relaxed her. It'd always been her first love, with nursing a close second, of course.

"In a minute. But first—" he captured her hand and angled his head toward the sofa "—let's sit a second."

Tressa studied their joined hands as they moved across the room. A simple act of kindness should not have felt so damn good. A soothing sensation tingled in her palm. At the sofa, Roth released her hand and guided her down, taking the spot next to her. The way he eyed her made her feel as if she'd sneaked the last piece of key lime pie, and he was simply waiting for her to confess before he had to accuse her.

Tressa straightened her back to give some semblance of strength. "Is everything okay?"

He leaned forward, rested his elbows on his thighs and intertwined his fingers. "You tell me."

Tressa arched a brow. "I…don't…know what you want me to say." Though she had a good idea he wanted her to mention something about what had taken place at The Underground. She'd hoped to avoid discussing her disastrous engagement party, but it seemed she wouldn't get off that easily. Couldn't he have waited until morning when she'd got a decent night's sleep before he approached the thorny subject?

"You've had a rough evening. If you—"

"I'm fine, Roth," she said, pushing to her feet. Subtlety obviously didn't work with him.

Before she could stalk away, he captured her hand again. This time he didn't let it go when she sat. His large hand completely swallowed hers, but she loved the feel of his warm flesh caressing hers.

"You keep saying you're fine, but I don't believe you."

"And I'm not trying to convince you." Instantly, she regretted being so callous. But dammit, she didn't want to discuss what had happened between her and Cyrus. Especially with Roth, of all people. She was hurt, embarrassed and still processing it all.

Her cruel tone appeared to have little effect on him. That same sympathetic expression remained on his attractive face. They stared at one another for a long time. Roth refused to turn away, and so did she. It felt as if he were trying to peer into her soul, but it was too dark for him to see inside. Beyond his strict and unwavering gaze lingered compassion. Mounds and mounds of compassion. And a hint of pity.

Tressa bent to the idea and turned away. "Don't feel sorry for me, Roth."

"I don't. I feel sorry for the bastard who didn't recognize what he had."

Tressa brought urgent focus back to Roth, her eyes lingering briefly on his mouth before climbing to latch onto his draining gaze again. Was he the reason she wasn't feeling the all-out dismay Cyrus's betrayal should have caused her? She was hurt—and angry—but she also felt something else. Relief.

Roth's cell phone vibrated and she flinched. "You should get that," she said, seeing her opportunity to escape this overwhelming and confusing moment.

Without even pulling the device from his pocket, he said, "It can wait."

After a couple more seconds of buzzing, either the call rolled to voice mail or the caller hung up. Tressa couldn't help but wonder if it was the woman Roth had planned to spend the weekend with. Before she'd dozed off on the drive up, Roth had sent several calls directly to voice mail. A part of her was happy to be here, away from her own problems, but another part of her felt guilty for potentially causing some for Roth, and for ruining his plans. Even if the idea of him making love to someone else bothered her more than it should have.

"I appreciate what you're trying to do, Roth. I truly do. But I don't want to talk about it now. I just… I just want to get through the night. I just want to get through the night," she repeated.

Roth brought her hand to his lips and kissed the inside of her wrist. It was the most intimate and soul-stirring move he could have made. The energy delivered through the sensual and delicate act sent a shock wave of desire sparking through her system. Everything about being there with Roth felt so right and so wrong all at the same time.

Chapter 3

When Tressa had volunteered to *whip something up*, it didn't take long for Roth to discover that they had two totally different definitions of the term. While he'd suggested preparing peanut butter and jelly sandwiches—to which she'd laughed hysterically—Tressa had taken the reins and created a spread that looked as if it belonged in a magazine for culinary professionals.

How in the hell had she managed to turn generic grocery items—a block of cheddar cheese, a can of Southern biscuits, beef hot dogs, thin-sliced pepperoni, club crackers, kettle chips and French onion dip—into a work of edible art? She truly was amazing in the kitchen.

"*Wow.* This looks scrumptious," he said, his growling stomach loudly approving. "A nurse and a chef. How in the heck did that happen?"

"I grew up watching my family help others. My father was a policeman, my mother a teacher. I had aunts, uncles and cousins who were firemen, clergy, counselors, doctors, lawyers, you name it. If there is a position out there geared toward helping people, one of my family members held it. Now, my love for cooking…I got that from my Poppa. My grandfather," she clarified and beamed with pride.

Roth envied her, envied anyone who'd grown up surrounded by family. As a youngster, he'd dreamed of growing up, getting married and having a thousand kids. Somewhere along the way, that vision had faded. Tressa's voice snatched him out of his thoughts.

"Do you mind if we eat in front of the fireplace?" she said.

"Sounds good to me."

After arranging everything on the brown shag rug, Roth returned to the kitchen for two hard black cherry lemonades. It'd actually been Tressa who'd introduced him to the drink. He usually went for the harder stuff— whiskey—or the occasional beer. With her feminine wiles, she'd convinced him to try the sweet beverage when they'd both been at Alonso and Vivian's place at the beach. He'd got hooked. On Tressa and the drink.

Roth recalled that beach trip. Watching Tressa wade through the water in an ocean-blue bikini, her skin glistening under the rays of the sun, had been torture in its most pleasurable form. On several occasions he'd wanted to ignore the fact that she was seeing someone and seduce the hell out of her, but he'd resisted. Looking back, he wished he had taken a risk. Maybe it would have spared her some heartache.

"Earth to Roth."

Tressa's voice pulled him back to reality. "I'm sorry. Did you say something?"

"Yes. I asked if you could bring some napkins."

Roth grabbed a stack of napkins off the counter and fanned them through the air. "Got it." He passed her one of the bottles, then eased down next to her.

Tressa eyed him curiously. "Are you okay?"

"Yeah. Yeah," he repeated when she didn't look convinced. "I drift sometimes. Growing up in foster care, I rarely got privacy. Sometimes escaping inside my own head was my only refuge."

Damn. Why had he shared any of that? His past was typically something he kept to himself. Not because he was ashamed of it, but because the second people learned he'd been a foster kid, they showered him with unnecessary sympathy. He hated that with a passion.

"I was a foster mother to a six-year-old once. Jamison," she said absently. "I'll never do it again."

"*Wow.* That bad, huh?"

Tressa grimaced. "God, I made that sound so harsh and insensitive. Let me clarify. I wouldn't do it again because I grew so attached to him in the short time he was with me. Watching him leave was the hardest thing I'd ever had to do. I cried like a baby for days."

He'd picked up on Tressa's nurturing side the first time he'd met her. It was one of the things he found so attractive about her. Nursing was the perfect profession for her. "Why didn't you adopt him?" Roth asked out of curiosity. She seemed to have cared for the child.

Tressa stared into the crackling fire. "I wanted to."

"Cyrus? Is he why you didn't adopt Jamison?" Roth wasn't sure why he'd come to that conclusion, but when

Tressa faced him again he knew he'd been spot-on. He hated the man even more.

She slid her gaze back to the fire. "Pathetic, huh?"

Roth wanted to say something encouraging, but he couldn't find the words. Growing up, every single day he'd wished for someone to care enough to want to adopt him, but it had never happened. But Tressa could have been the answer to the prayers Roth was sure Jamison said every night. She could have saved him from the hell of the foster system. But instead, she'd allowed that bastard Cyrus to convince her to send Jamison back into…hell.

Anger swirled inside him. He wasn't sure if it was geared more toward Cyrus or Tressa. He took a long swig from his bottle.

"After two weeks without the sound of Jamison's laughter, I realized the mistake I'd made. I contacted the agency, but I was too late. A family was interested in adopting him. I know I should have been ecstatic he'd found a permanent home. I was and I wasn't." She shook her head. "I had no right to be upset. I'd had my opportunity and blew it. I was being selfish. Which is typically *not* me, might I add."

She'd redeemed herself.

"He would have been lucky to have you as his mother."

A lazy smile curled her lips. "Thank you, Roth. That was kind of you to say."

Tressa's lips parted, then closed as if she'd reconsidered what she was about to say. The move drew his attention to her mouth. A knot formed in his stomach when he thought about how badly he wanted to lean over and kiss her. *Not a smart move. Fight this, Lexington.*

"I asked for a sign."

Scrambling his thoughts of ravishing her mouth, he said, "Excuse me?"

"Tonight. Right before you joined me on the balcony. I asked God to send me a sign if I was making a mistake by marrying Cyrus."

Was she suggesting he'd been her sign? Something warm and prideful blossomed in his chest.

"I guess your fiancé's mistress crashing your engagement party was a fairly obvious one, huh?"

And just like that, it wilted. "You don't seem too distraught about it." Roth pressed his lids together. "*Shit.* I'm sorry. That was an insensitive and stupid thing to say. I'm sure you're plenty upset."

"I'm not, actually. I mean, I'm angry as hell and hurt, but not in a debilitating manner, if that makes sense."

He hadn't expected that response. "Why?"

A beat of silence played between them.

Tressa lowered her head as if to hide her face in shame. "Because deep down, I knew Cyrus wasn't the right one for me. I just hung on in hopes of my feelings changing. I guess I kinda brought this whole mess on myself."

Roth knew it was a statement that didn't need a response, so he remained quiet. Before he'd even realized what he was doing, he draped an arm around her shoulder and pulled her against his chest. Tressa rested against him without any hesitations. Maybe he couldn't have her in the way he truly wanted, but he could be a friend in her time of need.

* * *

Tressa tossed and turned, unable to find a comfortable position. When she moved, it felt as if she were stuck to the smoldering leather. Kicking the quilt off that Roth had given her, she sat up and dragged the back of her hand across her forehead. It had to be three thousand degrees in here. And since heat rose, she was sure Roth was cooked to a crisp.

She sent a gaze to the loft. Though her view was obstructed, she imagined him sprawled out across the bed, his body sweat-dampened and glistening. A tingle in her belly slowly traveled to the space between her legs. As usual, her body was clearly on a mission to destroy her.

The popping embers brought her attention to the fireplace. She thought about their time in front of it earlier and how Roth had pulled her into his arms, and how safe she'd felt there. He'd wanted to kiss her, she was sure of it. So why hadn't he? Because he was too much of a gentleman.

She'd wanted Roth to kiss her, do more than kiss her, and it irked the hell out of her that he hadn't. But it'd probably been for the best. What kind of woman wanted a man to seduce her mere hours after finding out her fiancé has been sleeping with another woman? *A woman out for revenge*, she thought to herself.

No, that wasn't it. She blew a heavy breath. Her desire, need, want for Roth, weren't fueled by any of those things. Her longing for him was as authentic as it got. Which is why she had to fight it.

Tressa allowed her head to fall back against the cushions. Why did she always choose the wrong men? That included Roth. She wanted to believe he was a good guy, but the fact he could so easily push one woman aside—

who probably believed she had a position in his life—for another, even if the other was her, suggested otherwise.

Pushing everyone else aside, she focused on herself. "Will I ever find love?" she whispered to the universe, a tear sliding out the corner of her eye. "True love." That kind of ridiculous love that made you suddenly smile for no reason at all. She deserved that and wanted it. Wanted a husband who loved her beyond words. Wanted a family, a house full of kids—biological, adoptive or both. She wanted dogs, family dinners, vacations. "I want it all," she mumbled.

"You got it."

Tressa bolted forward to see Roth standing at the edge of the stairs in a navy blue tee that hugged his solid frame nicely and navy-blue-and-white pajama bottoms that sat just right on his lean frame. "What?"

"Insomnia?"

Tressa laughed at herself and wiped her eyes. "Um... sometimes. I didn't wake you, did I?"

"Ah, no, you didn't. I have trouble sleeping sometimes, too."

Roth studied her. No doubt he wanted to address her tears, but she prayed he wouldn't. Then, as if he'd read her mind, he turned his attention to the kitchen.

"Hot cocoa usually helps. Would you like some?" he said.

Although she teetered on the edge of spontaneously combusting, she said, "Sure." She could use the conversation, as long as it wasn't about her.

When she rose, her muscles protested the move.

Roth chuckled. "So, how's the sofa? Hate me yet?"

"Ha ha." Making her way across the room, she said, "Can I help?"

"No." Roth pointed to the small dining table. "Sit, woman."

Tressa saluted him. "Yes, sir."

Lounging in a chair, Tressa gleefully watched Roth move about. There was something alluring about a man working in the kitchen, especially this man. Even if all he was doing was heating milk.

Roth chatted about something, but truthfully, she had no idea about what. Lost in her own thoughts, she chuckled when she recalled the animated expression on his face when she'd nixed his PB&J sandwich suggestion.

"Don't laugh. It could happen," Roth said.

Breaking free from her thoughts, she said, "Um… what exactly could happen?"

He rested a hand on his hip. "You haven't heard a single word I've said, have you?"

Tressa bit at the corner of her lip and shook her head. "Sorry. I drift off sometimes."

He barked a laugh. Obviously, at the fact she'd used his own words against him. "Prepare to be impressed." He approached the table with two steaming mugs, set one in front of her, then lowered into a chair next to her at the square table with his in his hand.

Tressa took a sip and moaned. "*Mmm.* Real milk. And the cinnamon is a delicious touch. You did well."

"See, I can do a little something-something in the kitchen, too."

She imagined he could do a lot of something-something elsewhere, as well. After taking another sip, she said, "So, what is it that could happen?" Referring to his comment from earlier.

Roth's eyes slid to his mug, but only briefly. "While you're here with me, I plan to cater to your every need."

This sobered Tressa rather quickly. Cater to her every need? The possibilities made her stomach flutter and her body bloom. God, she prayed her nipples didn't bead underneath the oversize T-shirt Roth had given her to sleep in.

Scattering the illicit images hijacking her thoughts, she lowered her eyes to the steam rising from her cup. "Why—" She cleared her throat. "Why would you want to do that?"

"Because you deserve it. You've been through a lot. I think you need to be reminded that you're still a queen. And queens get served." He tapped her foot playfully with his own.

Tressa dared her body to give one damn indication of how much his words had affected her. Finally, someone saw and acknowledged her worth. But why did it have to be the man she was determined to resist?

Roth continued, "Plus, something tells me you never really abandon nurse mode. That you're constantly taking care of others and rarely focus on yourself, doing what makes Tressa happy."

Doing what makes Tressa happy. That should become her new motto. She shrugged one shoulder. "I like helping people," she said, in lieu of confessing that he was 100 percent correct. She rarely took time for herself.

"This weekend… It's all about you, lady. Got it?"

Roth crossed one ankle over the opposite knee, rested his hands in his lap, tilted his head and eyed her as if asserting his authority. She propped her elbow on the table, rested her cheek against her palm and eyed him back.

That seemed to be their thing—staring at one another for long, heated moments.

"Got it." What else could she say?

"Good."

Roth was a lethal combination: successful, sexy, charming. And he used it all well. Though a future with him was impractical, was a night of passionate, no-strings-attached sex out of the question?

What the hell was she saying? Roth struck her as the kind of man who molded into your system and stayed there, the kind of man who made women lose their minds. *One night?* Something told her one night with him would spiral her out of control. Her world was topsy-turvy enough. Still, everything about him intrigued her. *Stay away.*

Tressa circled her finger around the rim of the mug, ignoring his alluring aura. "I apologize if I caused any problems between you and your weekend companion." A corner of Roth's mouth lifted and her eyes fixed on his lips. Had anyone ever told him how damn sexy his mouth was? She was sure they had.

"Don't apologize," he said.

"I ruined your plans."

"Shit happens."

"Yes, it does." And there was some other *shit* she would love to happen right then.

Shit like him leaning over and kissing her long and hard.

Shit like him gliding his large hands up her bare thighs and underneath her shirt.

Shit like him pushing her panties to the side and curving two long fingers inside her.

Yes, all of that.

"Drifting again?" Roth said in a low, sensual tone.

Straightening her back, she said, "Um…why do you ask?"

Roth's eyes lowered to her chest and lingered there several seconds before rising. "Seemed as if you were… daydreaming."

The prickle on her skin told her she would regret looking down, but she tilted her head forward anyway. Yep, regret. Blazing-hot, flesh-searing regret.

There was no hiding those high beams of her beaded nipples. If she could have utilized one superpower at that very moment, it would have been the ability to make herself invisible. She pushed to a stand, urging the floor to swallow her. "I'm really tired. I'm…" Instead of finishing her thought, she forced her feet forward and willed her body to deactivate like she was a Transformer.

"You haven't finished your cocoa."

"It worked." She forced a yawn. "I don't think I need any more."

"Wait," Roth said.

Tressa froze as if he'd pointed a gun at her. When he moved toward her, she felt a wave of nervous tension. His head pointed toward the stairs. "Take the bed. I'll take the sofa."

As tempting as the offer was, she shook her head, then snuggled back onto the sofa.

A beat later Roth climbed in behind her. "Anyone ever told you you're too damn headstrong sometimes?"

Tressa stilled, her body going berserk from Roth's closeness, his solidity, his heat, his scent. Processing it all scrambled her brain. Her nipples tightened even more, her breathing grew clumsy, the space between her legs throbbed and begged to be touched. Sparring with her out-of-control body, she glanced over her shoulder and said, "Many call it being passionate. And what do you think you're doing?"

"If you're on the sofa, so am I. We suffer together."

"Roth—"

He made a snoring sound, which made her laugh. "Okay, suit yourself. But I'm not moving. I've grown very fond of this sofa. It's extremely comfortable. And for the record, no one falls asleep that fast."

Another round of snores caused her to laugh again.

Who was being the headstrong one now? If he wanted to stay there, then so be it. But there was no way she was getting off this sofa. Not because she was trying to prove how stubborn she could be. It was because Roth snuggled behind her felt too damn good to simply walk away from.

Chapter 4

While Tressa showered, Roth scrounged up something for her to wear shopping. He placed the T-shirt and sweatpants on the bed, then went back downstairs. Removing Juliette, he went out onto the deck to free his trapped emotions through music notes. He played and played hard. A rigid and rough tone that would be considered too edgy for most. This soothed him.

Several minutes later he stopped abruptly and snatched the instrument from his lips. He deserved every damn bothersome emotion swirling around inside him. The harder he tried to deny the pull Tressa had on him, the stronger it became, like a spiteful monster taunting him with its power over him.

If he had just allowed Tressa to get out of his SUV at the hotel, all of this could have been avoided. Why had he brought Tressa here?

Dammit. He was losing control. He never lost control.

The scene from that morning played in his head—waking up with Tressa fast asleep in his arms. For an hour he'd simply watched her sleep, not moving a single muscle and risking waking her. She felt right in his arms. Too damn right.

At one point he'd been so damn hard he was surprised he hadn't pushed her off the sofa. And when she subconsciously ground her ass against him, he thought he would die a slow and painful death. One thing was for sure, he didn't stand a chance in hell against Tressa Washington.

He was good at hard and cold. So why did he keep dispensing soft and warm around her. *Cater to your every need?* Had he really said that shit? He chuckled. *Yep.* And the funny thing about it, he'd actually meant every word.

He raised Juliette to his lips again but reconsidered. With the mayhem inside him now, playing would terrify the wildlife.

Tressa was right here. Right here for the claiming. Why was he hesitating?

From the deck, he heard her cell phone vibrate again. The tenth time in the past hour. Cyrus's no-good ass, no doubt. Tempted to answer the phone and tell the bastard to never call Tressa again, Roth resisted. Hell, for all he knew she wanted him to keep calling. She hadn't actually taken any of his calls to tell him otherwise. Wouldn't that have been the logical thing to do?

Wow. Wasn't that the pot calling the kettle black? He hadn't exactly jumped to take India's calls, either. Well, at least she'd had the good gumption to stop calling, obviously realizing he'd rescinded her invitation to the cabin.

Venturing back inside, he stored Juliette, then fixed himself another cup of coffee while he waited for Tressa so they could go to the store. Roth chuckled. Tressa's presence was definitely going to shock the hell out of Glen. He hoped the man didn't jump to any conclusions. He and Tressa were just friends. And that was how it had to remain. At least for now. At least until he was sure she was over her ex. And right now he wasn't so convinced that she was.

Tressa and Roth arrived at The General Store. Tressa originally assumed it was what Roth called it, but that was actually the name. The General Store. Couldn't get more generic than that. The airy barnlike structure resembled something from an old Western movie from the outside, but the inside was anything but old-timey.

Everything occupied the large store, including clothing. That was great because, though she was grateful, Roth's baggy St. Claire Aeronautics T-shirt and oversize black sweatpants didn't exactly make her a walking fashion movement. Nor did the stilettos she wore with it. And the mountain jacket swallowed her whole. But that part was okay, because Roth's scent saturated it. It was like having his warm arms swaddled around her all over again.

Her thoughts went to waking in his arms that morning. She couldn't recall ever experiencing a more peaceful night of sleep—well, until Roth started flinching in his sleep. Whatever he'd been dreaming kept him active.

Falling asleep on the sofa with Roth was one mistake she would not make again. The lapse in judgment had pushed her body to the brink of sexual insanity. Stubborn, passionate, whatever you wanted to call it, that had definitely been one battle she hadn't picked wisely.

"Lord, look who the mountain lion done dragged in."

Tressa followed the raspy voice to a short, round man. His long-sleeved denim shirt was buttoned all the way to the top and tucked into a pair of faded jeans held in place by green suspenders. With a head full of wiry salt-and-pepper hair, the older man kind of reminded her of her grandfather. God rest his soul.

A very docile dog with paws the size of saucers ambled up to Roth and brushed against his pant leg in the same manner an adoring cat would do. Roth rubbed his large head. "What's up, Shank?"

Shank's appreciation of the attention was clear, his back leg pumping harder the more Roth rubbed him. If Tressa hadn't known any better, she would have sworn the dog had smiled.

Tressa hung back while Roth, the gentleman and Shank socialized, but she could hear their conversation.

"Nettie told me you were coming to town. Since you're gonna be here a week, make sure you stop by for supper before you leave. You know Nettie will be hurt if you don't."

"I don't think I'll get by this trip. I'm only here for the weekend."

Confusion crinkled the man's aged dark brown skin. "I thought Nettie said you were here for the week."

Roth clapped him on the shoulder. "Change of plans."

Was the change because of her?

"Well, shucks. It's probably for the best. They're calling for snow Monday. Could be a headache." For the first time, his swamp-green eyes trailed to Tressa. "Or romantic. 'Pends on how you view it, I suppose. Hello, beautiful." He brushed past Roth.

"Glen, this is my friend Tressa," Roth said.

Tressa wasn't sure why Roth's use of the word *friend* bothered her, because it was exactly what they were. Friends. Just friends. "Hello." She offered her hand, but Glen pulled her into an embrace that suggested they'd known each other for years. *Okay, then. A hug it is.* Unlike with Roth, Shank had little interest in her and disappeared behind the counter.

When Glen held her at arm's length, his round cheeks blossomed. "Well, it's a pleasure meeting you, friend Tressa." Glen cut his eyes in Roth's direction. "And any friend of this man's is definitely a friend of mine."

Tressa noted Glen's obvious admiration for Roth.

Glen continued, "I know you haven't gone through all of that food my Nettie took to your place." He clapped a hand on Roth's shoulder. "My wife likes to make sure this joker is taken care of. And when she heard it might snow…she packed like a famine was coming." Glen sounded a huge laugh that made his stomach jiggle.

Ah. Nettie was Glen's wife. The information sent a hint of satisfaction through her.

"Nettie left plenty," Roth said. "We just need to gather a few other things."

The front door chimed, drawing their attention.

"All right. Well, holla if you need me," Glen said and moseyed away.

Tressa glanced up at Roth. "You were supposed to stay a week?"

He shrugged. "Yeah, but it's—"

"It's not okay." Normally, he was the one finishing her thoughts. "Don't let me disrupt your plans again. I already feel bad enough. We're staying the week. I, for one, wouldn't want to disappoint Nettie."

Roth laughed. "You did hear the part about snow, right? We could get stuck here beyond a week. Frankly, I'm not sure I can put up with you for more than a week."

Tressa's mouth fell open, and she swatted him playfully. "How rude."

"I'm just kidding. You're great company."

She was in no rush to get back to Raleigh. The more time she could spend in Silver Point, getting her thoughts together, the better. "I'm okay with getting stuck here. I have nothing better to do."

Roth folded his arms across his chest. "What about your job?"

"Twelve days on, twelve days off. I'm in my twelve-days-off stretch. And I don't start new culinary classes until the spring." Man, she was really pleading her case. And for the first time, she considered that maybe Roth's plans had changed because he *hadn't* wanted to spend a full week with her. Backpedaling, she said, "But you're probably right. Staying a week is probably a bad idea." When Roth laughed, she shot him a disapproving look. "What's so funny?"

He shook his head. "Nothing."

"What?" she repeated, adding a hint of bass to her voice as if it would force this rugged man to yield to her demand for information.

"You're delaying the inevitable, Tressa," he said plainly.

Delaying the inevitable? Inwardly, she sighed. Of course, they were back on the engagement party again. "I'm not delaying anything, *Roth*. I'm—"

"Running?"

Tressa shot him a narrow-eyed gaze. "Excuse me?"

He flashed his palm. "You know what? It's none of my business."

"You're right. It's not any of your business. So please stick to designing airplanes and refrain from trying to analyze me." She rolled her eyes and stalked off. *Running? Ha.* The nerve of him to make such an outlandish assessment simply because she wanted to enjoy the beauty of the mountains. Just like a damn man.

Running.

She wasn't running from anything. She planned to face her situation head-on, but not until *she* was ready.

A few steps from Roth's SUV the lights blinked twice, letting her know he'd unlocked the vehicle. Yanking the door open, she hurled herself inside. A second later the doors locked and Roth activated the auto-start feature. It wasn't long before warm air blew through the vents, and she closed them in protest, then laughed at herself. The only one who would suffer if she froze to death would be her.

Why was Roth so damn considerate? Why was he being so damn nice to her? It made it that much harder to be angry at him. And why was she so annoyed with him anyway?

Because he's right. She was running.

She'd ignored every phone call, text message, email and IM Cyrus had sent her. But she didn't have to explain herself to anyone. If she wanted to refrain from adulting for a while, it was her choice. No one else's. She glared toward The General Store. Not even to the man who'd altered his life for her.

Tressa closed her eyes and allowed her head to ease

back. Pressing two fingers against her temple, she attempted to knead the pain away. What was going on with her? She was usually more in control than this, a warrior. Now she simply felt like a battered peasant.

She chastised herself for not at least grabbing a piece or two before storming out of the store. Now she would have to wear the same outfit the entire weekend. Well, it served her right for being so juvenile.

Time ticked by. Why hadn't Roth emerged yet? Was he waiting for her to return? Recalling how she'd reacted filled her with regret. He clearly had her best interest at heart and had told her what she needed to hear, whether she wanted to hear it or not. Wasn't that what friends did for each other?

Friends? Could she even classify them as friends? Acquaintances probably worked better. How about potential cuddle buddies? This made her laugh.

Roth finally exited the store, carrying several overstuffed bags. When he opened the back door, a gust of cold air rushed in. He unloaded his haul, then slid behind the wheel.

"I grabbed you a few things," he said.

Grabbed her a few things? "You don't know my size."

"Twelve."

Or maybe he did. She tossed a glance in the back seat. A few things? It looked as if he'd outfitted her for the entire month. Even after she'd treated him like crap, he'd still looked after her. Who was this man? "Thank you," she said in a low, yielding tone. "I'll pay you back."

"That's not necessary." He sighed. "When you stormed off, I had to make an executive decision about what to get. You probably won't be runway ready, but you'll be warm."

God, she felt horrible about how she'd acted. "Roth—"

"If you're going to apologize, don't. I was out of line. You're a grown woman. You don't need me to hold your hand."

Maybe she did. Maybe that was exactly what she needed. For someone to simply hold her hand.

"I have this overwhelming need to protect you," Roth said.

The words almost seemed painful for him to admit. Had she just got a glimpse at a vulnerable Roth Lexington? The flash of weakness was endearing. Her lips twitched, but she didn't want to smile. Just like him, she needed to play it cool. But the fact that he wanted to protect her melted her heart into a big, messy puddle. No man had ever said anything like that to her. How did she respond?

Roth continued, "Big brother instinct. At least that's what my foster brothers would call it." Roth blew out another breath. "I should be the one apologizing. From this point forward, I will mind my own damn business. You have my word."

Big brother instinct? Was he suggesting he saw her as a kid sister?

Hell, no. No man would look at a sibling the way he looked at her.

"Still, I overreacted. You didn't deserve that. I'm sorry."

Roth studied her for a moment before he spoke. "I accept."

They fell into comfortable silence, staring at one

another in *their* way. She needed to give this thing they did a name. Something with fire in it, because every time they latched onto one another in one of these passion-swirling stare downs, flames burned through her as hot as lava.

Before she was completely consumed, she searched for something monumental to say, something that would convey her sentiment, a line that would reveal some things, but conceal others. Unfortunately, her brain was fried.

Chapter 5

Roth stood staring out at Silver Point in the distance, recalling the conversation he'd had with Tressa that morning outside the general store. He'd given her too much. Why in the hell had he told her about his need to protect her? *Way too much.* But what he'd seen in her eyes suggested it'd been just enough. For her, at least.

Why did this damn woman leave him feeling so exposed?

Tressa's reflections danced in the glass as she moved down the stairs. He wanted her in the worst way. There was truly no more denying that.

Tressa stood at the door alongside Roth. "God, this view is amazing. You can see the entire town below." When he didn't respond, Tressa glanced up at him. "Hey, are you okay?"

He flashed a low-wattage smile. "Sorry. I drifted off."

They shared a laugh at their inside joke.

"So, what do we have planned for this gorgeous Saturday afternoon? Now that I have clothes that fit— perfectly, I might add—I'm down for whatever."

"Whatever, huh?" That was a risky statement.

"Yep," she said with confidence.

"Well, let's get out of here, then." He had the perfect outing. And the more time they spent *out*, the less time he'd spend daydreaming about being *in* her.

Twenty minutes later they entered the Blue Ridge Parkway. The drive along this stretch was stunning, even with the leafless trees and absence of color. Hands down, fall was Roth's favorite time of year here with the vibrant reds, yellows and oranges.

Taking a quick detour, he veered off to the Grand-view Overlook. Tressa stood staring out at the miles and miles of rolling mountaintops, clouds swooping low as if they were there to welcome the formations into heaven.

"If I'd known how beautiful it is here, I'd have come a long time ago," Tressa said.

While Tressa took in every inch of the scene surrounding them, he took in every inch of her. Everything about her was so delicate, yet alluded strength. Definitely strong willed. He laughed to himself. It took a helluva woman to have gone through what she had and still be able to smile as bright as the sun. He admired that about her. That resilience. It was attractive as hell.

"Come on," he said, leading her back to the SUV. "If you liked that view, you'll love where we're headed next."

The road leading to the top of Grandfather Mountain was narrow, winding and steep. When they made it to the top, Tressa blew out a sigh of relief. He remembered his first time taking the trip and understood her reaction. "What's wrong?"

Tressa rested her hand over her heart. "A couple of times I thought we'd topple over the edge. Especially when another vehicle was coming from the opposite direction. I feel like I should get out and kiss the ground."

"You were never in any danger." He glanced into those tender eyes. *Turn away, man. Turn away.* Tressa's eyes were like puddles of brown desire that chipped away at the fortress around his heart every time he peered into them. At this rate she'd reach his center in no time. That troubled him. His heart was off-limits. Even to Tressa.

Exiting the vehicle, they stood in the parking lot for a moment, appreciating the view.

"Those houses look like they're sitting right on the edge of the mountain. One bump and *boom*, they're tumbling to the bottom." She leaned forward as if to gauge exactly how far they were from the bottom. A ways.

Roth decided to not mention the fact that if she looked up from town, his cabin would appear the same way.

When they finally made their way to one of the mountain's main attractions—the Mile High Swinging Bridge—Tressa mounted a protest. "No way, no how are you getting me on that." She jammed a finger at the metal structure. A passing couple laughed and she shot death rays at the backs of their heads.

"Trust me. It's not as bad as it looks," he said.

"No, it's probably worse. I don't do bridges. Not since—"

Her abrupt stop made Roth curious about what she was holding back.

"I don't do them, and no way in hell would I ever do a *swinging* bridge. *Swinging*, Roth. That means it moves, right?"

"Yes, but—"

She tossed her hands up. *"No way. No how. Let's go."*

When she tried to walk away, Roth hooked her by the waist. It was faint, but he swore Tressa moaned. Or maybe it'd been him. Damn, he hoped it hadn't been him. But it was possible. Touching her always triggered something in him. He willed himself to let go, but his arm didn't budge. "Baby, you can't—" He stopped abruptly. *Shit.* Had he really just called her *baby*? Releasing her, he took a step away.

Tressa turned to face him, a look of uncertainty in her gaze. Clearly, he'd spooked her with the accidental use of the term of endearment.

Clearing his throat, he started again, this time dropping *baby*. "Um…you can't come all the way to Grandfather Mountain and not cross the bridge. It's… sacrilegious."

Tressa studied him. "Okay. I'll do it, but on one condition."

"Name it." Because, really, how bad could it be?

"We stay in Silver Point the entire week."

Real bad. What she considered a condition, he considered a blessing. However…there were forces greater than him at work here, and those forces suggested he not tempt fate any more than he already had.

"I know you think I'm running, Roth. I'm not. It's

just that being here with…" Her eyes moved away briefly. "I feel at peace in Silver Point. I haven't felt this way in a long, long time." Her lips curled slightly. "And I kinda like it and selfishly want more."

How in the hell could he argue with that? "Okay."

"Really?"

Like him, she obviously couldn't believe his answer, either. He nodded.

"Good. Well, then…let's do this." Tressa stopped shy of taking the first step onto the bridge. "And you have to hold my hand."

This was getting worse and better by the second. He splayed his gloved fingers and Tressa locked hers with his. It was a damn good thing there was a barrier between their hands. From experience, he knew their current would have surely fried everyone on the bridge.

Tressa's grip on his hand tightened when the bridge swayed. It wasn't a vicious movement, but it could be felt. For a moment he thought she'd pull away and run back to steadier ground. But surprisingly, she kept soldiering forward.

The farther they walked, the more hesitant her steps became. Then she stopped.

"Wait, wait, wait, Roth. I've changed my mind. I don't want to do this. I can't…"

Her voice cracked as if she was about to cry, and what he saw on her face was genuine fear. They backtracked, went straight to the vehicle and headed back to the cabin. Tressa didn't utter a word the entire drive, simply stared out the window and bounced her legs in quick succession.

As bad as he wanted to, Roth didn't push her to talk. When she was ready, she'd tell him what had frightened her so much the color had drained from her face. Roth didn't know what had happened, but he was convinced it hadn't been anything good.

Damn. Had he pushed her too hard? He should have respected her wishes.

It was a little after six in the evening when they pulled into the driveway. Inside, Tressa removed her gloves, coat and hat, then eased onto the sofa and hugged her knees to her chest. Everything inside him wanted to go to her and cocoon her in his arms, protect her. Instead, he lit a fire.

"Can I get you anything? Hot chocolate, maybe?" he asked.

Tressa shook her head. "No. I'm sorry for ruining the day."

Roth eased down next to her and took her hand into his. "You didn't ruin anything. I had a *great* time." Simply because he was with her, but that part stayed with him.

"Yeah, until I spazzed out."

"That was my fault. I shouldn't have pushed you."

Tressa swallowed hard. "When I was a child, I spent summers with my grandparents in the country. One day my childhood best friend, Cammie, convinced me to go with her to The Spot."

"The Spot?"

"A place where all of the *cool* kids hung out."

For some reason Roth got the feeling this story wouldn't end well.

"We were only ten and shouldn't have been hanging out with sixteen-year-olds, but we thought we were grown."

Didn't all kids at that age?

"It was all a lure. The cussing, smoking, drinking." She chuckled. "Of course I was always the one too scared to do any of it. My grandmother didn't play. She was old-school and wholeheartedly believed in ass whoopings."

At sixteen, he'd done all of those things she had mentioned. However, he wouldn't have classified himself as a *cool* kid. More like a menace.

"I begged Cammie to leave, but she wanted to stay. 'Just a few more minutes.'" Tressa's grip on his hand tightened as if she remembered something awful. "This boy Cammie had a crush on, Kevin Marshall—" she said the name with a scowl "—convinced her to jump off the bridge and into the river below, which wasn't a big deal. Everyone did it." Her voice cracked as she continued.

Tears welled in her eyes.

"Cammie hit the water wrong. By the time anyone got to her, it was too late."

A tear slid down her cheek, and Roth brushed it away. A second later he draped an arm around her shoulders and pulled her against his chest. Tressa wrapped her arms around him and held on to him tightly.

"It was twenty-four years ago, but when I got out on that bridge, it all came rushing back."

Roth stroked her arm. "You have no idea how horrible I feel for forcing you out there."

"You didn't force me, Roth. We made a deal, which I assume is void now."

"Nah. I'll still honor it."

A beat of silence fell between them.

Tressa tilted her head to look at him. After several

beats of silence, she said, "Thank you, Roth. For everything. You're a good friend."

"You're welcome." And before he knew it, he'd pressed a kiss to her forehead. When she reared back, their gazes held.

For the thousandth time, he told himself this had to stop. All of it. Especially this thing they did, this silent, powerful connection. It was too invasive. If it continued, she'd be in a place no one was allowed. Not even her, especially not her.

"What do you see?"

Roth's brow furrowed. "What do you mean?"

"When you look at me that way, like you're trying to read my mind, what do you see?"

The question was loaded and dangerous. "A beautiful, strong, compassionate, selfless, intelligent, sometimes-stubborn woman, who I wish would have come into my life at a different time. A time when things were less… complicated." He'd fallen on his own sacrificial sword.

Tressa's gaze left him briefly. "I see," was all she said.

Forcing his eyes away from her hypnotic stare, he kissed the inside of her wrist. This was something he had to stop doing, too. But he did it again. Suddenly, her wrist wasn't enough for his lips.

His mouth covered hers in a slow, cautious manner. Maybe he was giving her the opportunity to pull away since he clearly lacked the ability to do so.

She didn't.

Instead, Tressa's lips parted to accept his greedy tongue. He probed every inch of her wet, delicious mouth. For months, he'd longed for this opportunity again, ever since he'd kissed her in her best friend's kitchen.

Then, just like that, he snatched his mouth away. What in the hell was he doing? She wasn't available to him. Not yet. Not in the way he wanted and needed her.

Staring into her uncertain eyes, he said, "I should start the stew." Amid great personal protest, he stood up and walked away, leaving her alone on the couch.

But being the sometimes-stubborn woman she was, Tressa didn't allow the conversation to simply end there. Perhaps because he'd said a lot, but had left even more unsaid and she wanted—possibly needed—to know what.

How did he tell her that after only a day with her, he was falling harder and faster than he'd ever fallen before, and *not* sound insane?

"You or me?" she said.

Roth avoided looking at her, despite his confusion by the question. "You or me?"

"Less complicated for you or for me?"

"For the both of us, Tressa."

"I see. Have you considered the possibility that this is truly simple, but we're the ones choosing to make it too hard?"

"Poetic, but what's real—"

"Are your feelings for me real?"

This brought his eyes to hers. His shoulders slumped, defeat fighting its way in.

"I thought they were. Mine are, too, Roth." She sighed. "Maybe a week here is not such a good idea, after all. You're right. This is complicated. We shouldn't risk things getting any more confusing or complicated for either of us." She stood from the couch. "I'll be ready first thing in the morning. If you don't mind, I'll take the bed tonight."

He stared at the back of her head as she climbed the stairs. Any more complicated? As if things between them could get any more complicated than they already were.

Chapter 6

The following morning Roth stared out the kitchen window and sipped his coffee. Just when he thought things couldn't get any more complicated, things got more complicated. His eyes swept over the snow-covered landscape. At least six inches had fallen overnight, and snow was still falling. Six inches. How in the hell was this even possible? The snow wasn't supposed to have arrived until tomorrow, not today.

Maybe Tressa had asked for a sign. He laughed to himself. *Signs*. This was a sign, all right. A sign that *shit happens*. And most of the time for the worst.

He massaged the tension in his neck. This was a complication. A colossal complication. Still, the snow was beautiful.

And speaking of beautiful things...

Tressa ambled down the stairs and he almost laughed

at the sight of her in the floor-length grandma gown he'd purchased at the general store. The plaid fabric did little to accentuate her assets, which had been his intent. Since the air was already tense between them, he kept his amusement to himself.

Boy, had she challenged him the night before. And what had he done about it? Not a damn thing. What he'd wanted to do was race across the floor, snatch her into his arms and kiss the hell out of her again. Let her taste and feel him. It'd taken all his strength to fight it. But he had.

Their kiss had left him exposed and put his feelings for her out there. Though he hadn't confirmed them, he hadn't denied them, either. *Lord, the balls on this woman.* Yeah, she was the type of woman who could ruin him or cause him to ruin himself.

"Good morning," she said, barely making eye contact with him.

"Morning."

Picking up the Not Before My Coffee mug she seemed to be fond of, she said, "I'm all packed. What time are we getting on the road?"

"That might be a little difficult," he said.

She eyed him for the first time since she'd come down and said, "Difficult?"

With a head tilt, he directed her to the glass door leading onto the deck.

When she slid open the thermal curtains, she gasped. "Oh. It's snowing. A lot."

The hint of excitement that danced in her tone made him smile.

Turning to him again, she said, "I thought it wasn't supposed to start until tomorrow."

Exactly what he'd thought, too. That was what he got for falling asleep on the sofa before the weather report aired. He shrugged. "Guess Mother Nature changed her mind. Unfortunately, going down the mountain is not an option for the next few days. Sorry."

"We're stuck?"

He couldn't readily decipher what flashed in her eyes. It wasn't anger, but not quite elation, either. "Don't worry. We're good. There's plenty of food, water and firewood. And if the power happens to go out, I have battery-operated lanterns." Of course, he doubted any of that impressed her, especially since she'd clearly been looking forward to leaving. Her words rang in his head. *I'm all packed.*

"You sound prepared." Tressa folded her arms across her chest and bit at the corner of her lip. "So, how long do you think it'll be before we can leave?"

"It's hard to say. Wednesday? Thursday? But you might luck out and can get away from me before then."

"I'm not trying to escape you, Roth."

"*Hmm.* Really? You seemed pretty determined to get away from me last night."

"I retreated. That's what people do when they're losing a battle, right?" She turned away and focused out the door again.

Well, she was right about one thing; there was a battle being fought, but she was wrong about who was losing.

"Do you have a sled?"

"A sled?"

She shrugged her flannel-covered shoulders. "Might as well take advantage of our situation, right? God, I miss playing in the snow."

A sled? "No, but I have trash bags. They work just as well."

For the first time since she'd come down the stairs, she smiled. "My friends and I used to use trash bags when I was younger."

"So did we." Mainly because no one he knew could afford a sled. He shuddered at those hard times. He never wanted to know how it felt to go without again.

"Do you want to eat first? I can whip us up something real quick."

"Later. After sledding—trash bagging."

They shared a laugh.

Okay, this was good. Laughter was good.

His eyes raked over her body. "Are you going to change? Could get a little chilly in places." *Damn.* Why had he gone there? He didn't need to add sexual innuendo to their already-delicate situation.

Tressa smiled in a way that suggested she'd caught the sly remark he'd tossed.

"Give me ten minutes," she said and left the room.

Roth pressed his palms against the countertop, leaned forward and shook his head. The logical portion of his brain warned him away, while the irrational part kept steering him toward Tressa. Either he stopped, or he would crash and burn.

Moments later, the sound of Tressa descending the stairs pulled him from his thoughts.

"Okay, I'm ready," she said.

Even wearing a black toboggan, black earmuffs, a black mountain jacket zipped up to her chin and black subzero gloves, she was breathtaking. Grabbing his winter gear and the bags, they headed out the door.

Outside, Roth squinted against the blinding landscape. Snow still fell in a steady shower of plump flakes. The crisp air burned his nostrils on inhale. Too long out here and he'd be a Popsicle.

When Tressa slid her hand into her back pocket, his eyes lowered to her butt. That plump rump filled those jeans nicely. His imagination took hold, warming him rather nicely. A stir below the waist forced his gaze away.

Lines of heated air danced like smoke clouds in front of him when he said, "Be careful going down the stairs." He hadn't thought to salt them until now, when the risk of Tressa slipping and injuring herself became a factor.

At the bottom Tressa waved him on. "Go ahead. I need to fix my sock." She knelt and fiddled with the black all-terrain boots she wore.

The second he moved past her, a snowball clocked him in the back of the head. "Ouch." He turned, nursing the area where he'd been hit.

Tressa covered her mouth and bent at the waist in laughter.

"Oh, you think that's funny, huh?" When he scooped up a glove full of fluffy snow, Tressa's eyes widened and the laughter ceased.

"You wouldn't."

He stalked toward her like a lion that was seconds from pouncing on its prey. "Oh, I would."

"But my snowball was the size of a gumdrop. Yours looks like a bowling ball."

"Don't fault me for having large hands." Large hands he wanted to use to explore every inch of her body.

"But…but…I owed you that."

Roth didn't bother asking her why she felt she owed him a snowball to the back of the head. Instead, he kept stalking toward her. If they were playing eye for an eye, he owed her, too. Owed her big. Owed her for making him experience all these crazy and confusing feelings.

The snow crunched under her feet as she took cautionary steps back. A beat later she took off running. "You won't take me alive."

Aiming, he chucked the snowball, hitting Tressa smack-dab in her left butt cheek. When it wiggled a little, he groaned to himself.

Tressa yelped, then grabbed her behind. "Ouch! That hurt."

"Oops," he said. "I was aiming higher. Really, I was." He'd have probably been more convincing if he'd have said it slipped.

Her face lit with laughter. "I'm going to get you for that, Roth Lexington."

"Take your best shot." He did a fake right, then a fake left.

For close to an hour, they ran around the yard like kids, blasting each other with snow. It was the most fun he'd had in years. This was how he wanted to spend his time with her. Having fun, not at each other's throats about a bunch of feelings.

"Time, time," Tressa said, forming snow-covered, gloved hands into a T. A blink later she fell back into a pillow of snow, flapping her arms and legs.

"Woman, what are you doing?"

"Making a snow angel. You have to make one, too."

She was crazy if she thought he was getting down there. "I'm not lying on that cold-ass ground. Have you ever heard of frostbite? Hypothermia?"

"Wimp."

Roth barked a laugh. "Name-calling won't force me to change my mind."

"Pretty please with a cherry on top."

All it took was one look into those spell-casting eyes. *Dammit.* "Okay, okay."

Roth wanted to pretend the idea of making snow angels didn't excite him, but it did. As a kid, he'd always seen it done on Christmas movies and had secretly wished it were him sprawled out in the snow, enjoying the time with his parents like the laughing children on the television.

"Closer, Roth. I won't bite."

A corner of his mouth lifted. Too bad. Biting could be fun.

"What just ran through your mind?" Tressa said.

"Um, how cold the ground is." His response sounded more like a question, rather than an answer to hers.

"Mmm-hmm."

She truly didn't want to know what had raced through his mind, what always raced through his mind when he was with her. Finding the nearest hard surface, and the ground would do to make love to her. By the time they left Silver Point, he'd need counseling.

They moved their arms and legs simultaneously. With angels formed, he made a motion to get up, but Tressa stopped him.

"Tressa, this ground is hella cold, woman."

"Two seconds." She reached into her pocket and pulled out her cell phone. "We have to take a selfie."

A selfie? He was freezing his balls off, and she wanted to take a selfie? "Are you serious?"

"Yes. Lie back and smile, you big brute."

Tressa positioned her head close to his. He had to

admit, onscreen they looked great together. After several snaps—some of them smiling, some of them making silly faces—Roth couldn't feel his ass.

"Three more and we're done," she said.

But before she could press the red dot on the screen, the phone vibrated in her hands. Cyrus's ugly mug filled the display. Roth snarled at the phone, then caught himself.

"I'll give you some privacy," he said. He'd wanted a reason to get off the hard, cold ground, and now he had one.

Tressa swiped her thumb across the screen, sending the call to voice mail. "I don't need it."

"Why?" Catching himself, he swallowed his words. After the general store incident, he'd vowed to mind his own damn business. "Can we get up now? I can't feel my legs."

"Quit complaining," she said.

A blink later Tressa smashed a handful of snow in his face. He heaved as if she was drowning him.

"Suck...er."

She tried to make a smooth getaway, but he was too fast. "Oh, no, you don't." He snagged the back of her coat, pulled her back and pinned her to the ground. Miraculously, his temperature rose several degrees.

Tressa squirmed and laughed as if Roth was tickling her. "I'm sorry. I'm sorry," she squealed, her laughter floating in the cold air.

"*Sorry* is not going to work. You have to pay for that. Do you see my face? My cold, wet face?" He scooped up a mound of snow and held it inches from her. "I'm sorry. This has to be done. It's going to hurt me more than it hurts you. But every action has an equal or opposite reaction. Any last words?"

Still rolling with laughter, she said, "Yes, yes."

"Okay. Spit them out before I exact my revenge."

Tressa laughed some more. "Revenge is best served cold."

Roth laughed, bringing the snow closer to her face.

"Wait. Wait. My last words."

His hand continued to close in on her. "You better make it quick."

Tressa sobered. "Kiss me."

Damn. He hadn't expected that. The expression on her face was firm, so he knew she hadn't said it by accident. "You don't want that, Tressa. If I kissed you, this time I wouldn't stop kissing you. Not until one or both of us froze to death out here."

"Death is inevitable. Wouldn't you prefer to die happy?"

Roth's jaw tightened. Did she have any idea how much delicious trouble teasing him could get her in? He tried his damnedest to pull away. Unfortunately, he lost all control. Lowering his head, he allowed his lips to brush hers. The heat that radiated through him burned hot enough to melt the snow off the entire mountain. "Are you sure this is what you want?" he asked against their sparsely touching lips.

"Oh, yeah. Kiss me, Roth Lexington. And kiss me like you mean it."

"And after the kiss ends?"

"We're both adults, Roth. It doesn't have to end at a kiss. One time or a hundred. I just want to be with you."

Roth growled at the implication, his erection swelling. *One time or hundred?* The thought was enough to make him shudder. He brushed his lips against hers again. "Do you know what you're asking for?"

"All of you. Now, enough teasing. Kiss me. With the same intensity you did last night."

"Okay," he said in a you've-been-warned tone. But before he could capture her mouth in the hellish manner he wanted, that damn cell phone interrupted them again. True, it could have been anyone in the world calling her, but instincts told him it was that rat bastard.

"Just ignore it," she said against his wanting mouth. "Kiss me."

The intrusion brought him back to his senses. He couldn't just ignore it. When he slowly pulled away from her, disappointment danced in her eyes. "You're not ready for me, Tressa. You have unfinished business. And every time you run from your fiancé—"

"*Ex*-fiancé," she corrected with unsubtle irritation in her tone.

"Is he really?" Roth regretted the terse response.

"You were there, Roth. You saw what happened, what he did to me. Do you really think I would still want to be with Cyrus after that? He's no longer a part of my life."

"Then you should quit avoiding the opportunity to tell him that, because right now he believes he still has a chance with you. And I'm not sure he doesn't. I'm not sure I'm not just your way of getting back at the man who wronged you."

Hurt filled Tressa's eyes and he knew he'd cut deep. He started to apologize but reconsidered. Yes, he felt horrible for hurting her, but as long as he kept this doubt wedged between them, things couldn't get out of focus again. He needed twenty-twenty vision to handle this situation.

Roth pushed himself from the ground, dusted the snow from his clothing, then offered Tressa his hand. Surprisingly, she allowed him to help her up. On her feet, her lips parted, then closed as if she reconsidered whatever she was about to say.

The next several hours were quiet ones. Tressa hadn't said ten words to him since they'd come in from the snow and he hated it. The silence was torture. Mainly because he enjoyed talking to her. It was always like a conversation with an old friend—unforced and effortless. Well, he guessed he could be grateful that she hadn't retreated upstairs.

Roth couldn't concentrate on the Walter Mosley novel he'd been reading, so he dog-eared the page and placed the book on the sofa beside them. He slid a glance at Tressa, whose eyes were pinned to the television screen.

Maybe he'd gone too far earlier. Who was he kidding? He'd gone way too far. Attempting to warm the frigid air around them, he said, "What are they saying about the weather?"

"It's snowing."

And the temperature in the room dropped several more degrees. Deciding not to poke the hornet's nest, he stood. "I'll start dinner." He waited to see if she would offer her assistance. Nothing. Yep, she was pissed at him. And she probably had a right to be. Again, he'd overstepped his boundaries. God knows he was the last person who should tell anyone how to manage their love life.

Tressa stood. "I'm really not all that hungry. I'll be upstairs if you need me."

Roth scrubbed a hand over his head and groaned. This woman was going to be the death of him. And judging by the amount of friction between them, something told him he wouldn't die happy.

Chapter 7

Tressa's eyes slowly peeled open, and she glanced at the clock on the nightstand. Three o'clock? Her brow furrowed. That can't be right. She'd only closed her eyes for two minutes. How in the hell had she slept for nine hours? *This damn mattress.* The plush pillow top made her feel as if she were sleeping on a cloud. It sure beat the hell out of that sofa.

The delicious aromas of onions and spices filled her nostrils, and her growling stomach instantly informed her she'd slept through dinner. Why hadn't Roth woken her to eat? Oh, yeah. She'd told him she wasn't hungry. She fell back against the cloud—mattress.

Their morning had started out great, then had turned into a damn disaster. She'd got so close to Roth, then just like that he'd pulled away. And why? Because he thought she was using him to get back at Cyrus. *Could he honestly believe that?* Even thinking he did frustrated her even more.

Being honest with herself, maybe a small part of her had wanted to feel as if she were getting a small amount of revenge against Cyrus. God, was she really this screwed up?

She released a humorless chuckle. Could she actually blame him for not wanting to get involved with her? Her life was a mess right now. Who wanted that kind of...*complication*?

A smile curled her lips when she closed her eyes and recalled their time in the snow together. They'd been having so much fun. Then Cyrus had ruined it. Disdain flowed through her. Cyrus was getting too good at disrupting her life.

She eyed the ceiling and replayed Roth's words in her head. *You're not ready for me. If you only knew how ready I am.* Why in the hell was he fighting this so hard? Oh, yeah. He believed Cyrus still had a chance with her. He was so far from the truth a compass couldn't have guided him back. Roth was right, she needed to talk to Cyrus. And she would. But for now, she'd make Cyrus wait for her to decide when she wanted to talk to him.

A thought occurred to her and she sat. One she should have seen before now. Roth wouldn't be intimidated by Cyrus. A man like Roth would welcome the challenge of claiming her for himself. Maybe a part of him did believe what he'd said. But there was more to it. Some other reason why she couldn't reach him. Something else he was hiding behind. But what?

A heavy sigh left her lips. Why should she drive herself insane trying to figure it out? He wanted nothing to do with her. She'd honor his wishes.

Just a few more days.

All she had to do was refuse to look into Roth's eyes, avoid sitting too close to him, quit appreciating his manly scent, stop enjoying the way her skin tingled when his dark eyes raked over her and keep her nipples from beading every time she thought about him caressing her breasts.

Yep, piece of cake. Which was exactly what she wanted now, Roth caressing her breasts and a piece of cake. Too bad she couldn't have either.

When her stomach growled again, she headed to raid the kitchen. She moved down the stairs like a cat burglar, but froze like an ice cube at the sight of Roth sprawled on the sofa fast asleep with an open book flat on his shirtless chest.

Whoa. Now, this was a sight for sore eyes, not-so-sore eyes, eyes of all states. The flickering flames washed him in an amber glow. It was the most alluring thing she'd ever seen. *Stop it, Tressa. Consider him the enemy. A well-put-together, devastatingly appealing enemy. But the enemy nonetheless.*

With his mouth partially open, soft snores poured out. Helpless against it, her eyes trailed over his smooth chest, appreciating the one pec peeping out from under the book. She would love to run her tongue over his nipple and those faithful-to-his-workout-routine abs. *No, you wouldn't.* Nor did she want those muscled arms to close around her in a snug embrace. *Nope. Not at all.*

A fine line of curly black hairs disappeared beneath the waistband of the gray sweatpants he wore. Her system hadn't been ready for the imprint at his crotch. She squinted to make sure her eyes weren't playing tricks on her. *Nope.* The man was packing, with a capital *P*.

Before the sight blinded her with desire, she slid her eyes away. A blanket lay in a multicolored puddle on the floor beside the sofa. Had it fallen off or had he kicked it off? Probably the latter. It felt like 710 degrees in there. In her case, she suspected the scorching temp had less to do with the fire and more to do with her reaction to all of that hot chocolate before her.

Tressa reached for the book, then reconsidered. Okay, now she was being silly. Even though he was now in the enemy category, what harm could come from her removing it?

The second she touched it, Roth's eyes popped open. In a flash, he grabbed a fistful of her shirt. Startled, her legs wobbled, then buckled, causing her to collapse on top of him.

The surge that coursed through her entire body had to be what it felt like to touch a live wire, minus the threat of certain death. Then again, by the magnitude of which her heart pounded, cardiac arrest couldn't be far behind.

Eyeing Roth dumbly, she said, "I… The book…" Her eyes traveled to his mouth, posed in a straight line. "I'm sorry." But when she tried to shimmy out of his hold, he held her in place.

As usual, they eyed each other for a long suffocating moment. Roth's eyes lowered to her mouth, and his jaw tensed as if he was fighting not just a desire to kiss her but a need.

His gaze rose to her in a manner that suggested he struggled with what to do next.

"Did I frighten you?" he said.

"Um…no."

"Why are you trembling?"

Desire. "Okay, maybe a little," she said instead.

"I'm sorry. I didn't mean to scare you. In one of the facilities I lived in for a while, you always had to keep one eye open. Falling asleep guaranteed you'd have your belongings stolen. I learned to sleep lightly. Some habits are hard to break."

"It's okay, really." To even imagine the hell he'd been exposed to growing up hurt her to the core. There was no wonder he didn't have a lot of faith in people. If she had to guess, he viewed her as one of those thieves in the night just waiting for him to doze off. But the only thing she would ever be interested in stealing from him was his heart.

Unsure why, Tressa rested her head on his shoulder. Maybe because she felt a tremble in him, too. Comforting the enemy was the noble thing to do, right?

To her surprise, Roth circled her in his warm, strong arms. She exhaled. *This is how it's supposed to be.* Closing her eyes, she relaxed and enjoyed being the object of his affection. This was how she liked things between them, comfortable, easy. So why was she about to make things bumpy?

"Something clearly exists between us, Roth. Something that gives me so much peace it scares me."

He hummed a sound that could have been interpreted as understanding or confusion, then his arms tightened around her a hint more. Was that his way of saying he felt the same way? She needed him to use words.

"Why are you afraid of me, Roth?" That was the only logical explanation. The only thing that made sense.

Roth chuckled a smooth, sexy sound that caressed her ears.

He placed a finger under her chin and tilted her head up. "Woman, do you really think I'm afraid of you?"

There was no need to be, but yes, she did.

"I'm not afraid, Tressa. Just cautious."

"Am I a risk?"

"Yes," he said without blinking.

Now they were getting somewhere. "Am I one worth taking?" She could tell by the way he studied her that the question had caught him off guard. Bringing her mouth within inches of his, she teased him in the same way he'd teased her earlier. "Am I a risk worth taking, Roth?"

His jaw tensed, relaxed, then tensed again. "Yeah, I think you are," he said in a low tone of surrender. "But it's not that—"

"It truly is that simple." Tressa pushed out of his arms and straddled him. She grabbed the hem of her shirt and lifted it over her head. Roth sucked his bottom lip between his teeth. His hardness swelled between her legs and pressed against her warmth. "Do you want to make love to me, Roth?"

"Yes." The sound of surrender danced in his voice.

"Good." And triumph danced in hers.

Lowering again, she glided the tip of her tongue slowly across his moist bottom lip, then dragged it between the split. He parted his lips and gently sucked her tongue into his mouth. They kissed for a long time. Slowly, tenderly.

Roth's hands explored her body, gliding up her arms, over her shoulders, down her back and came to rest on her ass. She moaned when he squeezed gently, then not so gently. The not so gently caused the throbbing between her legs to pulse even more ferociously.

She snaked a hand between them and rubbed Roth's hardness through the fabric of his sweatpants. A guttural sound rumbled in his chest. Venturing farther, she inched her hand beneath his waistband and wrapped her eager fingers around his hot, hard flesh and stroked gently.

In a swift move, Roth freed himself from her grasp. Like a child who'd been denied her favorite toy, she whined, "I want to feel you, Roth." She kissed one corner of his mouth. "I want to stroke you." She placed a kiss to the opposite side. "I want to bring you to the brink of exploding."

Roth didn't respond to her risqué words. Instead, he entangled his fingers in her hair, held her mouth to his and kissed her, hard and raw. Draping a strong arm across her back, he sat forward, shifted, swung his legs off the couch and stood.

When he took a step toward the stairs, Tressa broke their kiss. "In front of the fireplace. I've fantasized about making love to you there since we arrived."

Dark desire danced in Roth's eyes. Her head spun from the anticipation of being the recipient of the massive amount of passion she saw swimming in his hard stare.

Roth lowered them to the rug and blanketed her body. "I've craved making love to you since the very first time our eyes met months ago."

"That's a whole lot of bottled-up yearning."

"You have no idea." A corner of his mouth lifted into a wicked smile. "But you're about to find out." Roth pecked her gently, then stood.

"Where are you going?" she asked with shameless alarm in her tone.

"Nowhere, baby."

Tressa ogled with delight as Roth removed his pants. She gnawed at the corner of her lip, waiting for the fitted boxers to fall.

Roth hooked his thumbs inside the black fabric, then paused. "You're staring. Do you see something you like?"

Tressa sucked her bottom lip between her teeth and nodded seductively. At least in her mind she was being seductive. In actuality, she probably resembled a bobble-head doll. It didn't matter, as long as Roth gave her what she wanted.

Roth teased her, inching them down with no regard to speed. "Think you can handle it?"

"There's only one way to find out."

Tressa fought the urge to shout when Roth revealed himself. From the feel she'd copped earlier, she'd got a good idea of what to expect. But actually seeing his impressive manhood only thrilled her more. How much longer would she have to wait to experience it?

"I should warn you, I'm an unselfish lover. I like to give. And I'll keep giving until I'm sure you're satisfied."

Had he any idea how much his words turned her on? "I've never been known as a taker, but I guess I can make an exception and gracefully accept everything you're offering. That's the least I can do."

Roth smirked. "Close your eyes. And keep them closed until I say open them."

Her lips parted with mounting protest, but when Roth shook his head, clearly warding off her objections, she followed his directions. Once her eyes were shut, Roth blanketed her body again. The feel of his solid flesh meshed against her was foreplay all by itself.

Roth tilted her head to one side, then placed a delicate kiss just below her earlobe, then whispered in her ear, "All I want you to do is just feel. Can you do that for me?"

Oh, she was feeling already, so that shouldn't be a problem. "Yes," she said, mimicking his tone.

Roth kissed her in the same spot again. A blink later, what felt like hundreds of feather-soft kisses peppered her tingling skin: her neck, her jawline, her shoulder, her collarbone. Then it all stopped. Her lids fluttered, the desire to open her eyes as intense as the sensations swirling through her entire body.

Roth's soft lips tasted her skin again, kissing a line between the valley of her aching breasts. Dragging his tongue over one mound, he sucked a hardened bead between his lips. The intensity of the act caused Tressa to gasp, then smile with delight. He worked his tongue slowly, twirling circles around her tender nipple and flicking it gently. "Mmm."

He took his time exploring her body, kissing, licking, suckling, driving her mad. Inching down, Roth alternated between tender kisses and delicate nips to her skin. When he positioned her legs over his shoulders and claimed her core, she cried out in bliss. His tongue lit a raging blaze that threatened to consume her.

A bead of sweat trickled down her neck, taunting her already-sensitive skin. There was not one word that could effectively describe the havoc Roth was wreaking on her body.

As if he thought his tongue wasn't bringing her enough pleasure, he introduced his fingers. The second he glided them inside her wetness, curled them upward and worked them in and out of her, she lost all control. Fists clenched the soft material beneath them, blood whooshed in her ears and her body temperature rose several degrees.

Vicious waves of intense pleasure crashed through her. Never had she experienced an orgasm so powerful, so consuming. Her legs shook, her entire body folded to the delicious torture Roth was subjecting her to.

After what seemed like an eternity, her body calmed. Roth made his way back up her shivering torso in the same manner he'd gone down, still as gentle as before. He, again, feathered her burning skin with delicate kisses. His caring manner only made her want him more.

Roth's stone-like hardness pressed against her trembling thigh. At her mouth, he placed a soft kiss on her lips. The idea that her essence lingered on his lips aroused her again.

"Open your eyes," he said.

Beyond the heated look of desire, there was something more. Hesitation? She hoped not. If he denied her now, there was no doubt she'd die.

"Finish what you started," she said as motivation.

Roth reached for something. His wallet. Then a condom.

On his knees, their gazes held as he tore into the gold foil. She broke their connection in favor of watching him roll the latex down his impressive length. Her body supercharged at the notion of him satisfying the raging hunger inside her.

Roth blanketed her body and captured her mouth in a heady kiss. Without using his hand, his manhood effortlessly located her opening. She drew in a long, sharp breath, then released it in a shaky moan.

"Did you feel that, baby?"

Tressa whined, *"Yes."*

"Did it feel good?"

"Yes. Yes!"

Tressa couldn't ever remember a man filling her, stretching her, going as deep as Roth. And his gentleness... Sex with Cyrus had always been so urgent, so stiff, so swift. Not discounting the satisfaction obtained from the occasional urgent, stiff, fast interlude, because sometimes that was exactly how she wanted it, but this—the way Roth chose patient over rushed, gentle over rigid, unhurried over quick—was what she needed right now.

He'd wanted her to *just feel.* And, goodness, was she feeling.

She felt everything.

Passion.

Pleasure.

Delight.

Hunger.

Greed.

The clench of another orgasm.

Another.

What was Roth doing to her? Whose body was this? Multiple orgasms had never been a thing for her. And when she'd listened to her girlfriends boast about their back-to-back releases, she'd assumed something had been wrong with her. Now she knew better.

The orgasm tore through her far more potently than the last. Roth's name rolled off her tongue in a loud, pleasure-filled cry.

"Mmm." He hummed. "Say my name again, baby."

When he drove himself even deeper, she dragged her nails across his damp back. "Roth, Roth, Roth... Oh—I'm—"

More sensations swept through her, collecting the fragments the last release left behind.

Roth's rhythm increased but remained tender in delivery. A moan, groan, growl combination rumbled in his chest. A second later she felt him throbbing inside her. He stroked until he obviously had no more to give, collapsing next to her.

Their chests rose and fell in sync. Silently, he pulled her spent body into his arms. The soothing thump of his heartbeat lulled her. One thing was for sure. Roth knew how to make her feel like a woman.

Chapter 8

Roth catapulted himself off the floor, his heart hammering in his chest. Where the hell was he? Dizziness set in and he stumbled, but regained his balance before falling. Urgent eyes swept the room. The cabin. He was at the cabin.

Beads of sweat lined his forehead. Sucking in one lungful of air after the other, he still couldn't catch his breath. He bent at the waist, resting his sweaty palms on his knees. What the hell was—

"Roth?"

Though he recognized Tressa's voice, his brain couldn't process which direction it'd come from. "*Tressa.* I can't… I can't breathe," he said, dropping to one knee.

"I'm right here, Roth. I'm right here, baby. Just focus on my voice." Tressa knelt in front of him, cradling his face between her hands. "Just breathe. You're having a panic attack. Look at me. Come on. Look at me."

"I—" He heaved. "I can't—"

"Yes, you can. Just relax and look at me, Roth."

When he finally trained his focus on her, she took his trembling hand and placed it over her beating heart. The level *thump, thump, thump* had a near-instant calming effect on him.

"That's it. Just breathe. Slow and steady."

His brain shot on a hundred cylinders, but he processed her comforting tone. After several minutes he was back to normal—or as normal as he could be after something like that. Drained, plus somewhat embarrassed, Roth lowered himself to a seated position, propped his arms on his bent knees and lowered his head. Tressa moved behind him and kneaded his tight shoulders. Nothing had ever felt better.

"Bad dream?" she said in a near whisper, her words delicate.

"Nightmare." He scolded himself a second later. The door had just been opened to her questioning. And just as expected, she walked through.

"About?"

She continued to manipulate his tired muscles.

"Come here." Roth secured Tressa's naked body in his arms with one swift motion. His eyes combed over her ample breasts, and he fought the desire to dip low and suck one of her dark nipples into his mouth. His hunger stirred, but he tamed the beast.

A moment later his eyes slowly climbed to meet her gaze. He stared down into her sympathetic eyes. "Would you be upset if I said I didn't want to talk about it right now?" The unwanted memories that occasionally haunted his dreams weren't easily discussed.

Tressa fingered the cross around his neck. "Of course not." Her eyes slid to the pendant. "This is beautiful."

"It was a gift from a very special woman." *He* witnessed the flicker of confusion and/or concern on her face and flashed a half smile. "My ninth grade math teacher." He admired the piece. "I was actually pretty smart in school. Some would even say gifted. But I rarely applied myself, because no one ever influenced me to do so." Her expression turned serious. "Until Mrs. Sanders." Roth laughed. "She pulled me into her classroom one day, literally by my ear. She sat me down and said she saw something in me, something good. And that since I wanted to act like a wild mustang, she'd stay on my behind until I was tamed."

Tressa burst out laughing, then covered her mouth.

"Go 'head. Laugh at my pain."

"Sorry," she said through her fingers. "Continue, please."

"The next day Mrs. Sanders gave me this necklace. She said it was a reminder. A reminder that she and God would always be in my corner."

"Wow." Tressa blinked back the tears the powerful words summoned.

Roth brushed a stray hair from her brow. "Thank you, Tressa."

"For what?"

He captured the hand she'd used to place his over her heart and kissed the inside of her wrist, then her palm. "For sharing your energy with me."

"It was the least I could do. You gave me a lot of

your energy earlier." Her beautiful mouth curled into a delicate smile.

"Some moments from my past..." He paused. "I carry a lot of them with me, Tressa. It gets heavy sometimes."

"You carry the load well. You're one of the strongest men I've ever met, Roth Lexington. You may have gone through hell, but you managed to come out on the right side. Your past haunts you, but...I ain't 'fraid of no ghost."

Roth barked a laugh. "Beautiful, funny and sexy as hell." And one hell of a woman, because, in so many words, she'd told him she had his back.

"Yeah, you lucked out, sir. I'm the whole package. If I had a collar, I'd pop it."

Roth dragged an index finger down the center of her chest. "If you had a collar, that would mean you were wearing a shirt. I much prefer you butt naked and screaming my name."

"You up for showing me how much?"

"If you're up for taking it."

Tressa sat forward and hurried her mouth to his. He tried his damnedest to consume her whole. Roth avoided labeling what was happening between them. This powerful, intense, amazing chemistry that held him prisoner to her. Whatever it was, he prayed it never ended.

After experiencing the warmth of Roth's arms all night, Tressa didn't need to crack her eyes to know she was in bed alone. The chill confirmed it. Reaching for the sky, she stretched her tired muscles. She and Roth had made love in front of the fireplace several times, found their way to the bed and made love several more times.

Swinging her legs over the side of the bed, she sat there for a moment, recalling her night with him. A wide smile curled her lips. The smile dimmed when she thought about the panic attack he'd had. By the look on his face, he'd been embarrassed. He never had to be ashamed in front of her. Especially over anything in his past. The light and the dark moments, she'd embrace them all.

After a trip to the restroom, Tressa slid on one of Roth's shirts, tossing her nose up at the grandma gown he'd purchased for her at the general store and headed downstairs.

Roth was out on the deck, wearing nothing but a pair of pajama pants and a thin long-sleeved shirt. Was this the same man who'd nearly turned into a Popsicle when they'd played in the snow?

Strapping into her winter apparel—a toboggan, gloves, coat—and her boots, she joined Roth. The snow continued to fall in a steady shower, but not as heavy as the day before, suggesting it was nearing an end. The fact saddened her.

"Roth, where is your coat? You're going to catch pneumonia out here."

Roth bunched her coat in his hands and pulled her to him. Against her lips, he said, "I don't get sick," then kissed her senseless. Pulling away, he said, "Good morning."

It took a second or two for her brain to reboot after that spine-twisting kiss. "Good morning."

Tressa initially contributed the target warmth heating

her cheeks to her body's reaction to Roth, but then she noticed the black box affixed overhead. "What is that?"

Roth followed her stare. "An infrared heater."

"Huh." Why hadn't she noticed it before? Her attention slid to the stacks of colorful construction paper scattered on the tile-top table. "Is this arts and crafts hour?"

Roth barked a laugh. "No. I like making paper airplanes."

Considering his profession, that made sense.

"It helps clear my mind."

Tressa was tempted to ask him what had his mind cluttered, but figured it had something to do with his nightmare. Maybe soon he'd feel comfortable enough to talk to her about his past.

"Pick a color," he said.

She pressed her index finger into her chin. "Hmm." Then she settled on a steel blue color. Roth folded, tucked and creased before handing a fully formed plane back to her, along with a fine-point black Sharpie marker. "What's the marker for?"

"For writing a message on the inside of the plane."

"A message? What kind of message?"

"Anything you want."

Tressa hesitated for a moment, attempting to understand the purpose of this whole message-writing-on-the-plane thing. She laughed to herself. That sounded like a movie. "Who's going to read it?"

"No one."

Okay, now she was really confused. "We're writing a message that no one will ever read?"

"Yes. That's the beauty of it. It's like confession without the priest."

Roth scribbled something on his paper. She shrugged. What the hell. If no one was ever going to read it, what could it possibly hurt? *Hmm.* She tapped the marker against her bottom lip. What could she write? Something funny? Something ridiculous? A quote? *So many choices.* Her eyes slid to Roth. *Something intimate.* He had said it was like confession.

After she was done, Tressa refolded the paper, unsure if she should have written a love note to him. But the fact that no other human eyes would ever see it helped to put her mind at ease. "What now?"

"Now we exchange."

A hint of alarm rushed over her. "But you said—"

"Don't worry. I'm not going to read it."

A second or two passed as she debated whether or not to trust him with the plane. Reluctantly, she passed it over. "And now?"

"Now we throw them."

Before Tressa could even process what was happening, the steel blue paper soared through the air. Her mouth fell open and her eyes went wide in disbelief. "What— You— Why did you do that?"

A quizzical expression formed on Roth's face. "Do what?"

"Throw it." Her voice rose an octave.

Roth laughed. "That's typically what you do with paper planes." He flashed her a suspicious look. "What in the heck did you write on there, your Social Security number?"

That actually would have been better. "Um, an...old family recipe. It's top secret. I could be tossed out of the family for revealing it."

She bit back a laugh, but Roth didn't. He burst into laughter, then wrapped her in his arms from behind.

"Don't worry. Your recipe is safe. We're in the middle of nowhere, and bears can't read. I don't think." He kissed the back of her head. "Your turn, gorgeous. Just aim and fire."

It took a second, but she realized how ridiculous she was being and laughed at herself. Why was she so worried? Roth was right. They were in the middle of nowhere. Who did she think would come across her plane way out here? *No one*, she assured herself. *No one*, she repeated for good measure.

It was probably just lying out in the wet snow, waiting to be consumed by a mountain lion. Heck, even if someone did happen upon it, who would know it was from her? *No one.* Yep, that last *no one* made her feel so much better.

She released Roth's plane. *What did he write?* she wondered. Guess she'd never know. "Wow. Those little suckers sure did glide through the air."

"I hope your, uh, *recipe* wasn't too explicit," he said.

She wasn't sure she liked the sound of that. *Scratch that.* She was *sure* she hadn't liked the sound of that. "Why?"

"The last time I released planes, several made their way all the way into town. Imagine my surprise when I saw one pinned up in the general store. Good thing it was only a motivational quote."

Tressa's stomach dropped to her knees. "All the way into town, huh?" Her gaze slid through the trees and to Silver Point in the distance.

"Yep. I got skills. I'm reigning champ for longest distance and airtime in the Southeastern Paper Plane Competition. Skills." He kissed the back of her head again and pinched her butt. "I'll make us some breakfast."

Reigning... Paper Plane Competition? Forget food, she needed a shot of something strong.

Chapter 9

Roth lowered the book he'd been reading and peered over the top at Tressa sitting at the opposite side of the couch, engulfed in a Maya Angelou book of poems. He smiled. Man, she was engaged. The only other time he'd seen her this intense was when he'd sent her airplane sailing away the day before.

And speaking of airplanes... What in the hell had she written? Was it something about him? He recalled the way her body had tensed in his arms when he'd mentioned the possibility of her plane reaching town. Yep, it'd been about him.

He laughed to himself. That was presumptuous as hell, but he was rolling with it. "What did you write about me?"

Tressa's eyes slowly rose to his. "Excuse me?"

"On your plane. What did you write about me?"

Tressa placed the book facedown on her lap and folded her arms across her chest. "That's awfully presumptuous of you, sir."

"Well, ma'am, it's obvious you have a thing for me."

She tried to suppress a smile that broke through despite her efforts. Sobering, she said, "Oh, really?"

"Yep."

"And how, Mr. Lexington, did you come to this conclusion?"

"Well, Ms. Washington, first, it's the way you look at me."

She laughed. "And how do I look at you?"

"Like no woman has ever looked at me before. Like you truly see me."

Tressa's expression turned serious and so did his. The tender ways she looked at him revealed she saw something more than a vessel for sex.

"I do see you," she said. "Even the parts you try to hide."

And that was what he feared, her seeing the parts he wanted to keep hidden. He didn't want to scare her away. He also didn't want to give too much, too soon. Just in case. Throughout the years, he'd been used to far more things *not* working out than actually working.

Conversation seized, and they gaped at one another. Tressa was the first to break the silence. "You said *first*. Does that mean there are more reasons?"

There were, but did he want to list them? *What the hell?* "The way you touch me." He interpreted the expression on her face and answered the question before she asked. "Like you're trying to heal me, despite having no idea how deep my wounds run."

"I will."

"You will what?"

"One day I'll have an idea."

And she was probably right. Especially if he kept giving her pieces of himself. It was like he couldn't stop, like Tressa was meant to free him of some of the baggage he lugged around. Now seemed like the perfect time to ask an important question. "Should we talk about what's happ—"

"No," Tressa said.

Her tone held its signature levelness. The reply surprised him. He thought for sure she'd jump at the opportunity to discuss or define this beautiful magnetism. He arched a brow. "No?"

"We should just let it happen naturally. *Just feel.*"

"That's my line." And it brought back some damn good memories.

"Is it copyrighted?"

Roth lunged forward, blanketing Tressa's body with his. "Copyrighted? I'll show you copyrighted." He tickled her until she laughed so hard she snorted, which made him laugh just as hard.

Roth couldn't remember the last time he'd been so amused. He laughed so hard his sides began to hurt. By the time they settled, they both had tears running out the corners of their eyes. Instead of returning to his side of the sofa, he nestled against Tressa. She rested a delicate hand on his cheek.

"I see you, Roth Lexington, and I like the view."

He shifted his head to kiss her palm. "I'm not finished showing you who I am. Just be patient with me."

"Okay." She kissed the tip of his nose. "You're warm."

"Being this close to you makes my temperature rise," he said.

"Flirt."

Roth intended to kiss her, but before he made contact, Tressa pinned him with accusing eyes. "I think you're catching a cold."

He sighed. "Like I told you before, Nurse Washington, I don't get sick."

Several hours later Roth felt as if he'd been dragged up the entire mountain by a raggedy snowplow. Instead of Tressa saying, "I told you so," she instantly shifted into caregiver mode, forcing him upstairs and into bed, despite his protest.

He stared at the ceiling, bored out of his mind and lonely. "Tress… Baby, where are you? I miss you."

Damn. They'd only been apart twenty minutes. Plus, she was only a flight of stairs away. Yet, he missed her. Then it dawned on him. He didn't have a cold; he was experiencing symptoms of withdrawal. He laughed at the silly analogy. This was definitely a cold, and he felt like crap.

"Men are such babies when they're sick," she said, nearing the bed with a steamy bowl of something.

He pushed himself up onto his elbows. "What's that?"

"Chicken-and-rice soup."

He really didn't feel like eating, but she'd gone through so much trouble. To show his gratitude, he could surely get down a few swallows. "It smells delicious."

Tressa took a seat on the edge of the bed, scooped up a spoonful of the fragrant liquid, blew it to cool it down, then fed him.

"Mmm. Woman, you do have some major skills in the kitchen."

"Just in the kitchen?" A mischievous grin spread across her face.

Oh, if he had the energy—and a cootie-free status—he'd have taken her right there. "Tease."

After he'd got his fill, Tressa placed the bowl on the nightstand, butted her back against the headboard and directed his head onto her lap. She stroked a hand over his cheek. Why did her touch soothe him so much?

"Just rest."

Relaxed, Roth allowed his eyes to close. In his adult life, there had only been one woman he'd allowed his guard down around, and she'd hurt him. He'd sworn to never allow himself to be in that position again. And he'd managed to stick to his vow. Until now. Until Tressa. She'd become the exception to his ironclad rule.

With his ex, the connection had never been as strong as the one he felt with Tressa. Not even after the two years they were together. A part of him wanted—knew he needed—to pull away from this thing blooming between them. But the part of him that liked the way she looked at him, liked the way she touched him, loved how he felt when he was with her, beckoned him to stay, to risk.

"You're supposed to be resting, Mr. Lexington, not stewing in your thoughts."

"Huh?"

"I've noticed that whenever you glide your thumb back and forth across my skin like that, you're in deep thought."

Damn. He hadn't even realized he was doing it. He shifted to eye her.

Tressa smirked. "You're not the only observant one around here. I told you I see you. In vivid color." She winked.

Overwhelmed by the emotions storming inside him, all he could say was, "Oh, yeah?"

"Yeah."

Well, since she saw so much, did she see how hard he was falling for her?

The following morning, Roth was still fast asleep when Tressa snaked from the bed. She didn't readily move away. She watched him sleep. He looked so adorable.

Mr. I Don't Get Sick.

The nighttime elixir she'd prepared and given him—a mix of bourbon, because he had no rum, honey, lemon juice and cayenne pepper—had put him out cold. Recalling the expression on his face when he'd tasted the concoction nearly made her burst out laughing. It definitely wasn't the best-tasting remedy, but it worked wonders. He would feel like a new man when he woke up. Well...better than he did before he'd taken it, at least.

Moving away, she headed downstairs to prepare them some breakfast. Before making her way into the kitchen, she threw a few more pieces of wood on the fire. A glance out the window revealed the snow had finally stopped. *God, this place was gorgeous in the snow.* Probably even more beautiful in the spring when everything was in bloom. The idea of returning brought a smile to her face.

She'd got her wish to spend the week at the cabin. The only problem...Roth was sick. She shook her head at the quirk of fate. Actually, that wasn't all bad. Well, bad for him, but she actually enjoyed his relying on her. That built trust, which was the foundation of any relationship.

Collecting a few items from the fridge, she laid them out on the counter. They could remain at the cabin for several months and never run out of food. Mr. Glen's wife had stocked the place as if she'd been expecting a famine and didn't want Roth to suffer the fallout.

Nettie. Tressa laughed to herself. For a split second at the general store, she'd thought Nettie had been the woman Roth was supposed to spend the weekend with. That conjured another question. Who was the woman she'd replaced? And what had been their status? A friend with benefits? A booty call? An on-again, off-again lover?

Well, whatever was taking place between them was not just a passing fling. She was all-in and needed to know that Roth was, too.

Coffee. She needed coffee. Without caffeine, she never thought clearly. Abandoning the bacon and eggs, she brewed a pot of the morning roast. Once it was done, she poured herself a cup, leaned against the counter and trained her gaze through the window.

Enjoying how the first sip of the hot liquid pleasure warmed her nicely, she closed her eyes and moaned in delight. This would certainly help with clarity.

"I'm jealous."

Tressa opened her eyes to see Roth propped against the wall, watching her. How had she not heard him come down? His voice was raspy and his usually brilliant eyes weak. He still wore his pajama pants. Instead of a shirt, a thin blanket draped his shoulders. "What are you doing out of bed, young man?"

"I feel better. Not 100 percent, but much better than I felt last night."

He sneezed into the crook of his arm, paused, then sneezed again.

"Bless you." Nope, definitely not 100 percent. She felt so bad for him.

"Thanks," he croaked. Ambling to the sofa, he snagged a box of tissues and collapsed down onto the cushions. "My esophagus still burns from that poison you forced me to drink."

"I'm about to cook breakfast. Any special requests?"

He coughed, sneezed, then blew his nose. "I'm not really hungry."

"You have to eat something, Roth. Even if it's only a couple of bites of toast. It'll help you get your strength back."

"Yeah, I need my strength."

If she could see his face, she knew there'd be a roguish grin spread across it. She hated not being able to at least kiss him, but she didn't want the cooties, too, though her training told her she probably already had them. Maybe she'd better double up on the orange juice. They both couldn't fall ill.

"Okay. I request a couple of bites of toast," he said.

It sounded as if his face was buried in a pillow when he spoke. Even sick, he still found a way to make her smile. "A couple of bites of toast it is. And some orange juice," she added.

"And some orange juice." He peeped over the back of the sofa, then collapsed out of sight as if he didn't have the energy to maintain the position. "I'm supposed to be taking care of you, remember, beautiful?"

Tressa dropped four slices of bread into the toaster.

"You are taking care of me, handsome. You have been taking care of me since the moment you found me in your SUV."

Roth lazily chuckled. "I'm glad you chose my SUV to stow away in."

A smile touched her lips. "So am I."

After a hearty breakfast of bacon, egg, toast and juice for her—half a piece of toast and several sips of OJ for Roth—he fell asleep with his head in her lap. She used this time to continue the book of Maya Angelou quotes and poems she'd started.

Love is like a virus. Tressa snickered to herself. Maybe Roth didn't have a cold virus; maybe he was falling in love with her. *Wishful thinking.* With thoughts like these, she obviously hadn't had enough coffee. In her defense, the text did state love could happen to anybody at *any* time. *But after only a few days? Nah.* She wasn't buying it.

Then it dawned on her. This thing between her and Roth hadn't just grown wings at the cabin. It'd been soaring for months; she'd just chosen to ignore it. *Had* to ignore it. Her gaze lowered to Roth. "It took flight the moment I first laid eyes on you," she said in a whisper.

"What took flight?" Roth asked, his eyes still shut.

"*Um*…nothing. Just something I read in the book. Go back to sleep. You need your rest."

"And what do you need?"

Besides forever with you… "For you to get better."

Chapter 10

A day or so later, Roth felt almost back to normal. However, Tressa was still making a fuss over him taking it easy. He'd never had someone make such a big deal over his well-being. It felt...good.

The worst part of being sick hadn't been feeling like the tennis ball in a match between the Williams sisters; it was not being able to kiss Tressa in the deep, passionate manner he craved. He shot a glance toward the stairs. She'd been up there for an awfully long time. What was she doing? Taking a nap?

Pushing off the sofa, he climbed the stairs. When he heard Tressa on her cell phone, he stopped.

"*Fine.* I'll meet you. I have to go."

Her words were low but sharp and cold. That had to mean only one thing. It'd been her ex on the line. By her own words, they were done. So why had she agreed to meet him? A ping of jealousy rippled through him, followed by mounds of concern.

Taking a deep breath, he tried not to jump to conclusions. Continuing the climb, he said, "Hey." Tressa flinched at his words. He noted the look of distress on her face when she turned to him.

"Um, hey. Everything okay?" she asked.

"Yeah. Everything's fine." When his eyes briefly slid to the cell phone in her hand, she tossed it on the bed. "Everything okay with you?" A part of him wanted her to tell him she'd been on the line with her ex, while another part of him simply wanted to ignore what he'd heard and *trust* that there was no reason to be concerned. For him, trusting was far more easily considered than applied.

"Perfect, now that you're here."

Tressa closed the distance between them, wrapped her arms around his waist and rested her head on his chest. Her grip was snug, as if something had her rattled. What in the hell had Cyrus said to her? Anger tightened his jaw, diluting the emotions he'd previously felt. All he experienced now was that insistent need to shield her. He cocooned her in his arms, giving her the comfort he suspected she sought.

"Mmm. Your arms feel so good." She tilted her head upward. "How do you feel?"

"Like a new dollar bill. Thanks to your TLC."

"You know what would make you feel even better?"

Yes, he did. Making untamed, insanely hot love to her. But he decided to get her answer first. "What?"

"A hot bath."

Oh, he liked her suggestion even better.

Taking his hand, she pulled him toward the bathroom. As the tub filled, she poured several capfuls of rubbing alcohol into the water. This woman loved her rubbing alcohol. Since he'd got sick, she rubbed his chest down every night in the stuff. "Something my mother used to do," she said.

He didn't know if her home remedies actually worked, but between the rubbing alcohol and the potion she'd made him drink, he'd experienced very little chest congestion. Guess he couldn't discount them completely.

Stripping and climbing into the steamy water, he protested when Tressa said she wasn't joining him. Instead, she sat on the edge of the claw-foot tub, lathered a rag and began to wash his back. He hummed in satisfaction. "That feels amazing. A brother could get used to this kind of treatment."

"And a sister could get used to giving it to him."

When silence filled the room, he toyed with the idea of mentioning he'd overheard her conversation. Okay, eavesdropped, if one was being technical. Instead, he went a different route. "Have you talked to Vivian? You know she likes you to check in. I guess she wants to make sure I haven't fed you to a bear or something."

Tressa swiped the rag over his shoulders. "There's not a bear in North Carolina that can handle me."

Well played, he thought, considering how she'd craftily deflected his question. Maybe he was being a fool, but something deep inside him said he had nothing to worry about. He just hoped that *something* was right. "Really?"

"Yes, really."

"Well, this chocolate bear can handle you." In one swift motion, he had her in the tub with him. Her arms flailed as if she'd fallen into shark-infested waters.

"Roth Lexington! I can't believe you just did that. I'm soaked."

He closed his arms around her, causing her back to nestle against his chest. "Quit fronting, woman. You know you wanted to be in here with me."

"Whatever."

He could hear the smile in her voice. Tressa cooed as he pressed a kiss to her shoulder, the crook of her neck and the edge of her ear. "Thank you," he whispered softly. "Thank you for taking such good care of me."

Growing up in the system, he never got the luxury of homemade soup, specialty elixirs or back washes. And he sure as hell hadn't encountered anyone as selfless as Tressa. She was unlike any woman he'd ever bedded.

Bedded? That sounded so cold. Tressa wasn't just warming his bed; she was thawing his damn heart.

He honestly couldn't recall the last time anyone had shown him such compassion without wanting something in return.

Tressa glanced over her shoulder. "You are very welcome. Plus, I feel partly responsible for you being sick. It was my idea to play in the snow."

Now that she mentioned it… "Partly?"

"Ah, yes. *Partly.* I mean, you are a grown man. You could have said no."

Roth pinched her playfully on the thigh.

"Ouch," she said through laughter.

"As if I could have said no once I saw the way your face lit up. *'Ooh, snow,'*" he mocked.

She swatted him playfully. "I don't believe those were my exact words, and I definitely don't sound like that." Easing her head back against his shoulder, she smiled. "Snow reminds me of my grandmother. My father's mother," she clarified. "Gram used to make snow cream every snowfall. Never the first snow. The first snow washed away all the germs." She frowned as if the memory ushered in a great deal of sadness. "I miss her."

"How long has she…?"

"Almost six years. Old age. She was ninety-seven."

Roth whistled. "Ninety-seven. She lived a long life."

"A long and vibrant life. After my grandfather's death, she didn't sit around depressed and withdrawn. She traveled, she explored, she adventured, she fell in love over and over again. Though she once said she'd never love a man the way she'd loved my grandfather."

He kissed the back of her head. "Tell me about your grandfather."

She perked up. "My grandfather was as royal as a king to me."

She said it with so much passion Roth envisioned a *Coming to America* scene.

"He spoiled me and my brothers, but not with just material things. He spoiled us with knowledge and wisdom. He was a family *and* a community man. My grandfather was the man any and everyone in the neighborhood knew they could come to if they needed anything. Help with their mortgage. Help with utilities. Food for the dinner table. Clothing. School supplies for the kids. Anything." She sighed. "He's the reason I love to cook."

When Tressa blinked rapidly, he knew she was blinking back tears. He tightened his grip around her. "You're lucky to have grown up surrounded by so much love." He kissed the back of her head again. "You're so lucky. The only *l*-word I've ever truly known is loss. My mom died when I was three. My dad gave me to his sister to raise, then disappeared. When I was seven, my aunt died in a car crash. That's how I ended up in foster care. No one wanted me."

Tressa turned around to look at him. Tenderness blazed in her adoring eyes. "I want you," she said in a delicate voice.

"Why?"

She straightened and rested against him again. "Because this feels right. Us. We feel right. Things for me haven't felt right for a very long time, but this…this feels right. My life is not picture-perfect, Roth, but I really want you in it."

"The last time I…" He stopped short of saying *fell in love* in fear of spooking her. "I was hurt once. I've had my guard up ever since."

"What happened?"

"She cheated on me."

"Oh."

"From the start, I knew we hadn't been right for each other. But I wanted someone to love. And someone to love me," he added. "I entered into the relationship for all the wrong reasons. I wasn't the man I should have been. I was closed off and sometimes cold. She sought comfort elsewhere."

"And now? Are you still closed off and sometimes cold?"

"That was five years ago. I've done a lot of growing since then. I'm still a work in progress, but I'm here." Allowing his hands to glide up her body, he cupped her breasts and squeezed. "Don't you feel me?"

Tressa moaned a sound of satisfaction. "Yes," she said in a sultry tone. "I feel you all through my system."

Pinching her nipples through the wet fabric caused

her to shiver against him. When he rolled them simultaneously between his fingers, she moaned. "Woman, I want to kiss you so badly I can taste it. But since I can't right now, I'll find pleasure in making you come. Can I make you come?"

"O…kay."

After a couple more minutes teasing her taut nipples, he peeled the shirt from her body and dropped it into the water with them.

"You're not wearing any panties," he said, his tone laced with desire. "I like that." His hand snaked between her legs, gliding between her folds. When he started to massage her clit—first slowly, then with much more gusto—she gripped the sides of the tub.

"Yes, Roth. I want to come. Make me—"

She cried out, her body jerking forward. Water sloshed as if they'd activated jets. By the quickness of which he'd brought her to a climax, she'd wanted this. When she settled, her hand slinked into the water, her fingers wrapping around his painful erection.

"Shit," he growled through clenched teeth. She pumped up and down. Slow, then fast. Her grip tightened and a lightning bolt of pleasure sparked through his entire body. When her thumb swiped back and forth over the head of his shaft, he exploded.

His seed spilled into the water. Tressa continued to milk him. Several expletives flew past his lips as he throbbed in her hand.

Once they'd both gathered enough energy to move, they got out of the tub and moved into the bedroom to dress. Something had been missing from his life for a long time and he knew what. More like *who*. Tressa was that missing something. How did he know? Because he'd never felt so whole in his entire life.

Still, somewhere in the back of his mind, a tiny amount of doubt about whether or not she was truly over her ex lingered. But a relationship required taking chances, and he was willing to take one with Tressa. He just hoped he wasn't making a mistake.

Roth admired everything about this strong, vibrant, gentle woman. His gaze followed her around the room and watched as she dressed in a purple sweater and jeans. What he admired most about her wasn't the strength she displayed, her vibrancy or her gentleness. What he truly admired about her was her gigantic heart.

He'd always heard when you'd found "the one," you'd know.

He knew.

But despite all of that, all of the deep emotions she elicited, he still had to be cautious.

"What?" Tressa asked, a warm smile curling her lips.

He shook his head. "Nothing, beautiful. Nothing at all."

She neared him, then playfully tugged at his red long-sleeved shirt. "There's something. You just don't want to tell me. But you will." A look of triumph split across her pretty face, then she sauntered away.

Yep. The one.

Chapter 11

Tressa wasn't sure how she felt about leaving Silver Point. Usually when she traveled, her desire to return home grew after two days of being away from her own bed. But this time she wouldn't have minded a few more days at the cabin with Roth.

She eyed him as he locked up the cabin, then headed toward the SUV. The man resembled a sleek and sexy black stallion. When he opened the driver's-side door, the scent of his cologne rushed in and triggered all kinds of wicked memories.

"So, are you ready to explore Silver Point a little before we leave tomorrow?"

Tressa shifted toward him and bit at the corner of her lip. "Yes, but first…"

"I'm listening."

"I want to try the Mile High Swinging Bridge again. I think I'm ready."

Roth arched a brow. "You sure?"

She nodded. "As long as you're with me, I'm good."

"I'll be right there," he said, leaning over and placing a gentle kiss on her lips. "Let's do this."

Forty-five minutes later, they arrived at the entrance to Grandfather Mountain. While remnants of snow remained, their drive up the mountain was clear.

Instead of taking the stairs from the parking lot, they accessed the bridge using the elevator located inside the Top Shop. It felt as if the temperature had dropped several degrees from the time they'd left the cabin until now. She zipped her coat higher.

"You ready?" Roth asked.

Staring across the lengthy structure, Tressa experienced a brief moment of hesitation, then she glanced up at Roth and an instant calm washed over her. "Yes."

Roth splayed his fingers and she joined her hand with his. They took several steps until they were standing on metal. Her grip on his hand tightened.

"You know you don't have to do this, right?"

"I know. But I want to." Needed to, actually.

Several moments later, they stood in the center of the bridge. Though her heart thumped in her chest a little harder than normal, her temperature rose despite the cold and the slight tremble of her body. The 360-degree, panoramic view of the mountains was amazing.

She closed her eyes and inhaled the cool, crisp air, but popped them open when the bridge swayed harder than it had before. Gripping the rail, she gasped.

"You're okay," Roth said.

When they finally reached the opposite side, Tressa

blew a sigh of relief. Roth wrapped his strong arms around her, and it felt as if she'd been awarded a medal of honor.

"You did it," he said, lowering his mouth to hers.

They shared a celebratory kiss. Briefly, everyone and everything around them disappeared, and she forgot they were standing a mile above sea level. Her connection with Roth made her feel invincible. That's how she knew this thing they shared was real.

The trip back across the bridge was a breeze. You never would have known that just twenty minutes prior, she'd been a bundle of nerves. Making their way back to the car, Roth pulled her hand to his mouth and kissed her wrist.

"I'm proud of you," he said.

The simple affirmation lit her soul. "Thank you."

Once she was settled inside the vehicle, Roth rounded the vehicle and slid behind the wheel.

"I hope you don't mind, but I told Nettie and Glen we'd stop by for lunch. I hate coming to Silver Point and not spending a little time with them."

"I don't mind, but I look a mess. I need to change."

Roth leaned in to kiss her on the cheek. "Baby, you look fine. You always look fine, fully clothed or naked."

"Flirt."

He bounced his brows twice.

When they arrived at Nettie and Glen's place, Tressa admired the ranch-style brick home. A wide porch spanned the entire length of the front of the house. Four white rocking chairs rocked faintly against a bitter breeze. In the distance sat a barn and a stable. She wondered if there were horses inside.

Roth got out and rounded the vehicle. When her door

opened, a hint of nervousness fluttered in her stomach. For some reason she felt as if she was about to meet his parents for the first time.

"What's wrong?"

She imagined saying, "What if they don't like me?" in a whiny voice. Instead, she smiled and said, "I'm really going to miss Silver Point."

"We'll come back anytime you want." He placed a kiss on her forehead, then led her to the front door.

Glen made a thunderous sound of excitement when the door opened. If nothing else, the man was jolly. He gave Roth a manly handshake, then pulled Tressa into his arms.

"I'm glad y'all could make it. Come on in."

Glen stepped aside and they entered. Instantly, Tressa had her answer about whether there were horses in the barn. The spacious sitting room was like a horse museum. Cowboy hats, pictures of horses and horseshoes all claimed space on several walls. Horse figurines, medals and trophies were on display in a well-lit wooden cabinet.

Yep, there were horses. Or at least there used to be.

Tressa eyed a picture of a group of men posing at what looked to be a rodeo. Her eyes narrowed on one of the men in the frame. Though he was several years younger and several pounds lighter, the wide smile was unmistakable. *Glen.* Had the man been a cowboy in his youth?

"Yeah, that's me," Glen said as if he'd read her thoughts. "Sure do miss the thrill of it all. You ever been to a rodeo?"

Tressa shook her head.

Glen clapped Roth on the back. "You should take her, Pilot. She'd enjoy it."

When Glen moved away, Tressa mouthed, "Pilot?"

Roth leaned in close. "I don't just design planes. I sometimes like to fly them."

"Fly—"

Tressa's inquiry was cut short. She assumed the stocky woman who rushed toward them was Nettie. She wrapped her chubby arms around Roth and hugged as if squeezing him gave her life. With her short stature, she barely made it to Roth's pecs.

"I didn't think I'd get to see you this trip."

When Nettie finally released Roth, she set her eyes on Tressa, then Roth, then Tressa again. "Oh, Glen, you were right."

Tressa's brow furrowed. *Right? Right about what?*

Nettie didn't elaborate; she simply pulled Tressa into her arms and hugged her just as affectionately as she had Roth. One thing about Nettie and Glen, they sure knew how to make a person feel at ease.

Lunch consisted of the best stew Tressa had ever put in her mouth, homemade sourdough rolls and a lemon meringue pie that practically melted in her mouth. When Glen asked to see Roth in his study, Tressa and Nettie tidied the kitchen, then sat at the table and thumbed through Nettie's recipe box.

Tressa was like a kid on Christmas morning. Some of the recipes had been passed down through Nettie's family from generation to generation. Tressa made a stack of all the ones she wanted to photocopy. There was only one she wasn't allowed to even glance at. When she'd reached for the flimsy aged once-white paper, Nettie moved it out of reach.

"Tradition," Nettie said. "You have to be family for this recipe. Glen's mother passed this along to me when we were first married. She said every woman should own one recipe of love." Nettie beamed as if remembering the moment. "It's brought years and years of Sanders love."

Tressa's mind worked overtime, guessing what kind of recipe it could be. A beverage, appetizer, main dish, then she settled on it being a dessert. An extremely decadent dessert. *Fine chocolate, maybe? Orange liqueur? No, raspberry.*

Suddenly, something Nettie said replayed in her head. *Years and years of* Sanders *love.*

Nettie wasn't just the food delivery woman; she was much more. "Sanders? You were the teacher who gave him the necklace."

Nettie smiled. "He told you about that?"

Tressa nodded. "Yes, he did. I laughed at the mustang part," she admitted.

Nettie laughed. "Lord, that boy was a handful. Cutting class, fighting, getting into all kinds of trouble." She frowned. "Glen and I could never have kids of our own. My students became my kids and I poured as much love into them as I could. For some reason, I really took to Pilot, and he took to me."

"You saw something in him," Tressa said, repeating what Roth had told her.

"Yes, I did. He had both book and street smarts. There was no limit to what he could accomplish. He just needed someone to believe in him. We would have adopted him, but we could never cut through all of the red tape. Seems they based their decisions on the amount of money one has, rather than the amount of love."

"Thank you for believing in him." Tressa had said the words before she'd even realized her brain was forming them. But gratitude for such a selfless act was warranted.

Nettie cupped Tressa's hands. "Pilot must really like you. He's always been so guarded when it came to his past. Be good to him. You have an extraordinary man."

Nettie wasn't telling her anything she didn't already know. "I will."

Once they'd said their goodbyes and made promises to return soon, Tressa and Roth ventured into town.

Their first stop was the Silver Point Coffee House. When they walked through the door, Roth was greeted by several individuals. Obviously, he was well-known by the locals.

Just like The General Store, the coffeehouse gave an old-timey impression from the outside, but the inside told a different story. Exposed brick and aged wood gave the quaint shop a modern feel. There was ample seating with bistro and four-top tables scattered about. What caught Tressa's eye was the two oversize empty burgundy recliners positioned in front of a tall crackling fireplace. It was the perfect spot for them.

Roth joined her by the fireplace with two steaming soup-bowl-sized mugs of hot chocolate. "Wow. That's a lot of hot chocolate."

"They do everything big in Silver Point."

They sipped and chatted for hours. She couldn't remember the last time she enjoyed herself just talking. Roth told her about his time spent at The Cardinal House, a group home for boys, and she shared with him things from her childhood she'd never told anyone else. Like the time she'd broken the neighbor's window and her brother had taken the fall for her. He still held it over her head 'til this day.

When they finally left the coffeehouse, they ventured to the thrift store next door where Roth had purchased them several books. Their last stop was a unique card-slash-gift shop.

Inside the vehicle, Tressa pulled a small box from her purse and passed it to Roth.

"What's this?" he asked.

"Open it."

Roth lifted the metal bookmark from the wrapping. "Don't judge a book by its cover or a man by his past."

"It's not much. I just wanted to say thank you."

"For what?"

"For…everything. This week has been incredible, Roth. You have been incredible. You made what should have been the very worst week of my life, the best week of my life. I want you to know I appreciate you."

Roth reached over, placed his hand behind her neck and pulled her mouth close to his, but he didn't kiss her. Staring into her eyes, he said, "Thank you."

"You're welcome."

The following morning, Tressa and Roth finally got on the road back to Raleigh. Roth had been silent since they'd pulled away from the cabin. Was he regretting returning home, too?

The way he brushed his thumb back and forth across the steering wheel told her something occupied his thoughts.

"I'm really going to miss Silver Point," she said.

Roth didn't respond. He simply eyed her briefly, smiled and returned his gaze to the road ahead.

What was going on with him? She wanted to think the best—that things weren't changing now that they'd left the close quarters of the cabin. But the worst crept in—that just maybe she had been only a temporary replacement for Roth.

When they pulled into her cul-de-sac several hours later, the fact that Cyrus's car wasn't parked in her driveway brought her relief. Not that she cared if Cyrus saw her and Roth together. It was a well-deserved ass whooping she knew Cyrus would have surely talked himself into. She would have felt awful if Roth went to jail for assault on account of her.

Inside, Tressa watched as Roth took in his surroundings. His eyes moved from the open living room decorated in brown and teal, to the kitchen outfitted with stainless steel appliances.

"You have a nice place," he said, folding his arms across his chest.

"Thank you. Is everything okay, Roth? You seem to have something on your mind."

He directed her to the chocolate sofa. "Sit. We need to talk."

She wasn't sure she liked the sound of that. *We need to talk* were typically words of doom. "Okay," she said, ignoring the quiver in her stomach. She eased down and stared up at him. "I'm listening."

Roth took a seat on the leather ottoman directly in front of her and cupped her hands. She saw the signs. When he dipped his head, she decided to make this easier for him. "I get it, Roth. You're not ready for a commitment. You thought you were, but now…I get it." Her heart crumbled a little more with every word she spoke. "We had a great time at the cabin, but we're back in the real world and things don't look as clear for you, right? You just want to be friends." She forced a smile. "I get it and…it's okay."

Roth brought his gaze to her with urgency. "Can you let me go so easily?"

Now she was confused. Wasn't he trying to get away? "I don't want to let you go, but I don't want to hold on to you if you don't want to be held. I'm giving you an easy out."

"Giving me an easy out? I don't want an out. I was trying to give you one."

Her brows bunched. "Why would you think I wanted an out? I'm crazy about you, Roth Lexington. You have to know that by now."

Roth's head dipped again. "I heard you on the phone yesterday. You were agreeing to meet with someone. To talk things over. I assumed it was your ex."

Shit. He'd overheard her. Why hadn't he said anything before now? Well, he was half-right. She had agreed to meet with Cyrus, but only to give him all his junk she planned to pack up tonight. "I promise you, Roth, he's not the man I want in my life."

"Tressa…"

He paused as if whatever he needed to say pained him. Anything this difficult to declare couldn't be good.

"For years," he continued, "I've avoided romantic attachment like the plague. Being hurt once was enough for me. I was content with my bachelor lifestyle. Then you stowed away in the back of my SUV and forced me to whisk you off with me to my cabin."

"Forced? Really?"

"Whose story is this?" Roth said, followed by a lazy half smile.

"Fine. Carry on with your tall tale."

"Not many people have ever seen me beyond what I've wanted them to see. I keep trying to hide from you…" He sighed heavily. "I can't."

"Why would you want to hide from me, Roth?"

"You know how they say every man has a weakness?"

She nodded.

"You're mine. And honestly, I hate that shit, Tressa. You scare me. You scare me because you make me too vulnerable. Vulnerability gets you hurt. Vulnerability is a sign of we—"

She pressed a finger against his lips. "Vulnerability is a sign of being human. And being human looks excellent on you." She smiled but Roth remained stone-faced. "There's something you're not saying. What is it?"

"I need to fall back, Tressa. Not because I don't want to be with you. Trust me, I do. But I need you to be 200 percent sure I'm who you want."

Her heart sank to her feet. Where was all of this coming from? He wanted to be with her, but he wouldn't? It made no sense. How in the hell had things dissolved so quickly between them? "Roth—"

"Please, baby. It's hard enough letting…" His words faded. "Don't fight me on this."

Tressa snatched her hands away as frustration kicked in. "Don't *fight* you on this? You claim you want me, but it sure as hell doesn't feel that way to me. You asked me if I could let you go so easily. Can you let me go?"

When he didn't respond, she stood. "We spent an

amazing week together, one that I'll never regret, but obviously, you do. If you want to walk away, Roth, I'll let you. But you will not, *will not*," she repeated, "put your cowardliness on me."

When she tried to walk away, Roth placed his hands on either side of her waist to keep her from escaping. She blinked rapidly to keep her tears from falling. "I'm giving you *your* out, Roth. Just take it."

He didn't utter a word, didn't budge. Instead, he pulled her close to him and rested his forehead against her trembling stomach. She couldn't explain, but she could feel his fear as if they were one cell. Instinctively, her hand smoothed over his head to comfort him. This was one of the strongest men she'd ever encountered, but at that moment she truly believed she was his weakness. What she desperately needed him to know was she would also be his strength.

Lowering to her knees, she positioned herself between Roth's legs and cradled his face between her hands. A look of exhaustion played in his features. The sight clenched her heart.

Neither of them uttered a word. Words would have only bottled something too powerful to contain. Besides, none were needed. All that needed to be said was conveyed by a method they'd seemed to have perfected.

The stare.

That stare.

Their stare.

His eyes said he knew. And she was sure he saw the same knowledge in hers. Nothing was accidental. Where they were on this journey was exactly where they were both supposed to be.

Chapter 12

It'd been a week since she'd returned from Silver Point, and Tressa missed her time there already. She and Roth were still going strong, and she'd been the happiest she'd been in a long time. Every time she thought about him—which was quite often—her heart skipped a beat.

She glanced at the clock. Ten o'clock. A second later the house phone rang like clockwork. Without even looking at the caller ID, she knew it was Roth. He'd called her every day for the past week at the exact same time. Ten o'clock sharp.

"Hello," she croaked.

While it had taken a few days, she'd finally succumbed to Roth's cooties. In bed with a pounding headache, stuffy nose, congestion, a sore throat and a fever had not been how she'd envisioned spending her remaining time off.

However, there had been a silver lining to this dark cloud, and he'd waited on her hand and foot. Every morning he'd dropped by with breakfast on his way to work. Every day at lunch he'd either personally delivered or had food delivered to her. Every afternoon after a long day's work, he was at her front door ready to nurse her back to health.

Roth's smooth tone poured over the line. "Hey, beautiful. How ya feel?"

Tressa groaned. "*Ugh.* How do I sound?"

"Like a world-renowned opera singer."

"If you were trying to make me smile, it worked."

"That's always my goal," he said. "Have you had any of the remedy I mixed for you?"

"Um…yes. Several ounces, I believe."

Immediately, she asked forgiveness for the lie she'd just told. Roth had attempted to remake the home remedy she'd whipped up for him at the cabin when he'd fallen ill.

Unfortunately, what he'd brought to her bedside had been the color of dirty pond water and tasted like a lukewarm mix of turnip-green juice and hot sauce with a twist of lemon. But she'd taken several sips because he'd gone through the trouble of preparing it.

She made a note to pour a few ounces down the drain before he arrived later that evening. Had to keep up appearances.

"I wish I were there with you," he said.

"I wish you were here, too."

"I have several things here at the office I *have* to complete before I leave, then I'm all yours. Are you hungry? I can have something delivered."

She loved how this man took such good care of her. "No. My appetite is a bit wonky today."

"Well, get some rest and I'll be by tonight."

"You've been spreading yourself thin, Roth. Go home and get you some rest. I'll be fine. I am a nurse, remember?"

Roth chuckled. "Don't worry about me. And I'm perfectly aware of your profession, Nurse Washington, but I'll see you tonight anyway."

She wasn't going to argue. They said their goodbyes and Tressa snuggled against her pillow, wishing it was Roth's chest instead.

A beat later her cell phone chimed, indicating a text message. Eyeing the screen, she frowned. *Cyrus.*

Can't make the meet tomorrow. Something came up. Need to reschedule.

"Again, huh," she said to the screen, then sighed. This was the second time he'd squandered the opportunity to collect his things. Not giving him any more of her energy, she tossed the phone aside. She'd deal with him later.

Tressa got her wish several hours later when Roth undressed and slid into bed next to her. Despite her low-grade fever, his warm body was just the remedy she needed. She felt so guilty taking up so much of his time, but craved spending every available minute with him. She prayed this new relationship excitement never wore off for either of them.

Nestling under his chin, she wished she could smell his manly scent, but her clogged nose made it impossible. "I've missed you," she said.

"I seriously doubt more than I have you." Roth placed a finger under Tressa's chin and tilted her head upward. "Kiss me, woman. Just a little peck. I can't stand my lips not touching yours another day."

"You want my cooties?"

"Wasn't it you who told me I can't catch the same cold twice?"

"Yes, but we can't be certain you're the one who gave me this cold."

Roth's eyes narrowed in animated accusation. "Let me find out you've been out here, kissing other men and collecting their cooties."

Tressa kissed Roth under the chin, his five-o'clock shadow pricking her lips. "There is only one man's lips I'm concerned with. But I'm also concerned about his well-being. So…" She kissed the tip of her fingers and pressed them to his forehead, the tip of his nose, his cheek, then his chin. "That will have to do for now."

"I'll take what I can get, but just so you know, my lips are going to wither up and fall off if I can't kiss you soon. And not just your neck and shoulders."

Tressa laughed, which turned into a ferocious coughing fit. Roth retrieved the glass of water from the nightstand and offered it to her once she'd settled. "Sick sucks," she said, claiming her position back on Roth's chest.

Roth glided his hand up and down her back. "You'll be 100 percent soon."

Tressa closed her eyes, but remembered the package she'd received earlier. "I have a gift for you," she said, coming up with one elbow.

Tressa sent Roth to the kitchen for the package on

the counter. If there was one thing she was good at, it was one-click shopping.

Roth slid back into bed with her, then removed the crystals. "Um…you got me coal? Have I been a bad boy?"

She swatted him playfully. "They're called black tourmaline." One of her coworkers had told her the stone, along with amethyst, was supposed to help ward off negative energy. "It's a protective crystal. Place it by the bed, and it'll ward off nightmares. We'll keep some here and some at your place." Tressa ticked off the other benefits of black tourmaline: promotes detoxification, balances the chakras, relieves stress, improves mental alertness. "And there are a few more. I just can't remember them all. I think it's supposed to be good for memory, too. That'll—" She smiled when she saw the way Roth eyed her. "What?"

Roth's expression was unreadable. Was he trying to process all of the uses or was he thinking she was bat shit crazy? A second later he smashed his lips to hers. He didn't try to gain entry into her mouth with his tongue; he just held his lips against hers.

When Roth finally pulled away and looked at her, he didn't have to say a single word, but he did. "I've never met anyone like you. You are an amazing woman, Tressa Washington. Your heart…" He shook his head. "Come here." He pulled her into his arms again and lay back on the bed. "Woman, you're the answer to all of my unspoken prayers. I'm a damn lucky man."

And she was a damn lucky woman.

Roth glanced over at the black torpo… Black toma… The black crystals Tressa had got him. He didn't know whether or not he should put much stock into their powers, but the fact that Tressa had been thoughtful enough to purchase them gave him incentive. His heart had swelled even more from her kindness. When he'd said he was a lucky man, he'd meant every word.

He glanced down at her, fast asleep in his arms. Her hair was strewed, she didn't have on any makeup and she snored—loud. But in spite of all of that, she was the most gorgeous woman he'd ever seen. All he wanted to do was take care of her, protect her. In his head, he knew he needed to slow down, but Tressa made him want to move at the speed of light. His feelings for this woman grew more powerful every single day.

Lifting her arm, she squirmed but didn't wake. He gingerly snaked out of bed. If he fell asleep at seven in the evening, he'd pop up in the middle of the night, wide awake. Moving from the bedroom to the kitchen, he snagged a banana, laughing at the two monkeys climbing up the arm of the aluminum banana holder.

Though he'd probably not have been ambitious enough to choose the color, the pear-green-themed decor in the room played well with the cherry cabinets and stainless steel appliances. He wondered if she'd specifically chosen this house because of the spacious kitchen. Roth imagined her there at the oversize island, chopping, dicing, smiling as she prepared for him and their kids.

Their kids. He chuckled and washed a hand over his head. "Slow down, Lex," he mumbled to himself. There was no guarantee Tressa would give him the football team he wanted. At least six. Even more if she agreed. Possibly even adopt. There were a lot of kids out there who needed a good home and love. He had a lot of love to give.

Abandoning the thoughts of his imaginary family, he moved from the kitchen and into the living room and dropped onto the chocolate sofa. Grabbing the tablet he'd brought with him, he tapped in his pass code. *Might as well use the time to get some work done.*

With Tressa right in the next room, maybe he could actually focus with her so close. He laughed when he considered how one minute he could be positioned at the design desk in his office, working away, the next he'd abandoned all thoughts of work and had replaced them with Tressa.

Damn, that woman is potent. She was all woman for sure. But she was also a flame that blazed through him constantly. *A man on fire,* he thought.

Setting the tablet aside for a moment, he went back into the kitchen for a bottle of water. When he decided the banana wasn't going to be enough to hold him, he grabbed the bag of sour-cream-and-cheddar chips from the top of the refrigerator.

Taking the last paper towel, he moved to the storage room where Tressa kept additional rolls. A cardboard box sitting on the floor caught his eye. For whatever reason, he lifted the top and looked inside.

The box was crammed packed with male toiletries. Obviously, Tressa had got around to packing Cyrus's shit, but hadn't got around to giving it to him. The idea of her meeting with the weasel bothered him. No doubt the slimy bastard would try to slither his way back into her life. His jaw tightened, then relaxed. He wasn't worried about that loser.

Or should he have been? Would seeing him awake

any dormant feelings Tressa still had for the man? There had to still be some, right? Roth shook his head. He couldn't stress over that. He had to trust Tressa, trust what they had.

Replacing the top, he grabbed the roll of paper towels, dropped it onto the wooden holder, then returned to the living room. Instead of working, as he'd intended, he found himself scrolling through the pictures of his boys—young men, he corrected—from the community center where he gave saxophone lessons to disadvantaged kids. They had been so excited about performing for their families at the Duke Energy Center for the Performing Arts in downtown Raleigh. And not just the younger kids, but the sixteen- and seventeen-year-olds, too.

They looked all *GQ*'d, decked out in their tuxedos and fedoras. He laughed at some of the jailhouse poses. He planned to do all he could to make sure none of them ever found themselves posing that way in a real jailhouse.

"My bed gets awfully lonely without you."

Tressa ambled across the floor and he directed her onto his lap. Kissing the side of her head, he said, "I had intended to get some work done since you were sleeping, but I started looking at these pictures."

"There better not be any big-boobed blondes on that device." She managed a lazy smile.

"Jealous?"

"Maybe."

He nuzzled her neck, then kissed it gently. "Your big boobs are the only ones I'm interested in. And I can't wait until you're better so I can show you just how interested I am." Redirecting his wayward thoughts, he positioned the screen so that they both could see the images.

"Are these the young men in your saxophone academy?"

"Yeah. A good-looking bunch, huh?"

"Yes." Tressa pointed to one of the younger kids. "Aww, he's a cutie-pie. Those glasses make him look like a young philosopher."

"Sebastian. He's smart as a whip and doesn't miss a doggone thing. He's a little timid, but will say whatever is on his mind. No filter. He's a good kid, though."

Tressa swiped through the pictures, commenting on most of them. "God, I can't wait to have a house full of kids running around. It's going—"

Tressa stopped as if she'd realized a mistake she'd made. Maybe she thought the mention of kids had spooked him. It hadn't. They could talk about kids all night long, because as far as he was concerned, she would be the mother of his football team.

Chapter 13

Tressa usually didn't wake at the crack of dawn when she didn't have to work. But Roth had shown up at her door at six that Saturday morning—*six in the morning*—blindfolded her and whisked her away to an undisclosed location. At least he had the common courtesy to bring her coffee.

In the month they'd been dating, every day was an adventure with him. What she truly valued was the fact that he always made time for her. Whether it was whisking her off to dinner and a movie, or challenging her to a game of bowling. He truly made her feel like she was an important part of his life.

"Are we there yet, Roth?" Tressa tussled with the silky fabric over her eyes. "This blindfold is chafing me."

"Hands off," he said, swatting her playfully. "We're almost there."

A short time later Roth activated the turn signal and made a right. He parked, then moved around to her side of the vehicle and helped her out onto the hard surface. Where were they? Using her available senses, she tuned in to her surroundings.

She smelled…exhaust, maybe? No, gasoline. Definitely gasoline. A racetrack? No. If they were at a racetrack, she would have heard the roaring engines and cheers from a crowd. Plus, she seriously doubted anyone raced this early.

What did she hear? Wind. Lots of it. And she felt it, too. A windmill farm? That made her laugh. Why in the world would Roth bring her to a windmill farm?

Roth took her hand and led her forward. She remembered the last time he'd held her hand for support. The Mile High Swinging Bridge at Grandfather Mountain. That trip to Silver Point had been the start of something beautiful.

Tressa's steps were now just as hesitant as they'd been walking out on the bridge. "Don't let me fall, Roth." Although, she knew he'd never allow that to happen.

"Do you think I'd allow you to hurt a pretty little hair on your head? Stand right here," he said, placing his hands on both her shoulders as if to steady her. "Don't move."

"And risk breaking my neck?" Her ears perked when she heard what sounded like a key being inserted into a lock. Then it sounded as if he'd opened a metal garage door. It clanked and rattled so loud it startled her. She reached out, her wiggling fingers searching for the comforts of his. "Roth?"

"I'm right here, baby." He stood directly behind her. "You ready?"

"Been ready." When Roth removed the blindfold, her eyes adjusted to the light. Squinting, she blinked several times, but the small personal aircraft was still there in all its massive glory. "What…"

Roth placed his hand on her lower back and ushered her forward. "Meet *Zoom*."

Tressa's eyes scanned the black-and-silver plane, then the hangar where it was being housed. If it was any brighter in the all-white, pristine space, she would have needed sunglasses. *"Zoom?"* she said absently.

"You ready?"

She whipped toward him, confused by the question. "Ready for what?"

"Part two of your Valentine's Day. We'll only be gone overnight."

Still confused, she said, "Part two…?" Her words trailed off.

Part one of her Valentine's Day had been pretty damn fantastic. Roth had had four dozen red roses delivered to the hospital. When he'd arrived at her house to pick her up for dinner, he'd given her the largest box of chocolate she'd ever seen. After a dinner fit for a queen, they'd returned to his place and made love for hours.

"Where are we going?"

"It's a surprise."

Roth strapped her into the two-seater aircraft. She'd be lying if she said she wasn't a little nervous about Roth flying them to wherever it was he was flying them to. And it wasn't the fact that it was Roth, per se; she would have been nervous with anyone behind the wheel—controls—of this intimate craft. Plus, when she flew, she was used to having far more space, and far more pilots manning the controls.

"Um, is your pilot's license up-to-date?"

Roth flashed a stunned expression. "You have to have a license to fly? The video game simulation never stated that." He smirked. "Don't worry, baby." He cradled her chin, leaned over and kissed her gently on the lips. "I got you. A champion, remember?"

"Of flying *paper* planes." She hadn't actually meant to say the words aloud.

"Look at me," Roth said. When she did, he continued, "Not only do I always want you to feel happy with me, I want you to feel safe, too. If you don't want to do this, we don't have to. I won't be offended."

Tressa inhaled and exhaled slowly. "Let's do this."

Several moments later, they taxied down the runway, then ascended.

Tressa marveled at the view below them. The cars and houses resembled pieces in a board game. Roth seemed so comfortable, so at-home handling *Zoom*, that all of her earlier concerns melted away.

"How long have you had *Zoom*?" Tressa felt as if she was screaming into the aviation headset.

"I built her a little over two years ago."

Built? Okay, she hadn't heard that right. Adjusting her earpiece, she said, "Did you say *you* built this plane? Like…with a hammer and screwdriver?"

Roth laughed. "I had a few more tools, but yeah, something like that."

A second later she released a shaky chuckle. "You're not serious."

The look he gave her said he was. Who in the hell

was this man? More important, was he any good at building planes?

Roughly five hours later they touched down in Arizona, took an Uber to the car rental location, grabbed a bite to eat, purchased more temperature-appropriate clothing, then checked into the Renaissance in downtown Phoenix.

The spacious hotel room was decorated in blues and browns. A king-size bed rested in the middle of the spacious hotel room. A wall-mounted TV, a dresser and two nightstands outfitted the space. Their location boasted an amazing view of mountains in the distance.

"This bed is cozy. You should come and try it out," Roth said, sprawled across the plush mattress.

Tressa turned away from the window. One of the first things to catch her eye—excluding her man—were the black tourmaline crystals on the nightstand. He'd brought them with him. For some reason, it made her smile.

"Come over here, woman. There are some things I need to do—I mean, say—to you."

She moved toward the bed, slowly removing her clothing piece by piece. Roth came up on his elbows and sucked his bottom lip between his teeth, watching her eagerly. First, her shirt dropped to the floor, then her bra. Next, her jeans and panties. Raw desire danced in his eyes.

"I want that. All of that," he said, his heated gaze burning a line up and down her body.

In a seductive voice, she said, "And you can have it, baby. All of it." She smirked. "After I get a hot shower." She took off for the bathroom.

"Woman! Oh, you will pay for that."

A couple of hours and orgasms later, Tressa had been eager to stay in bed with Roth all day long, exploring new ways to please one another. Unfortunately, he'd insisted there was someplace they needed to be by seven, but he wouldn't give her any other details beyond that. What in the heck did he have up his sleeve? Whatever it was, she knew she'd like it.

On the drive to their destination, Tressa grilled Roth, but he remained tight-lipped. Thirty minutes later they crossed the line into Chandler, Arizona. A short time after that, a sign read Rawhide at Wild Horse Pass. "Where are—" Tressa's eyes widened when she saw a second billboard-type sign. Popping Roth in the arm, she said, "Arizona Black Rodeo?"

"Glen said I should take you to a rodeo, right? Here we are."

"No. I mean, yes. But no, I can't believe we're here." Tender eyes admired him. "You flew all the way to Arizona to bring me to the rodeo." Tressa's heart did a pitter-patter in her chest. "You're all right with me, *Pilot.*"

Hundreds of people appeared to be in attendance in the large arena. Tressa had never seen this many people dressed like cowboys and cowgirls in one place in her life. Young, old and everything in between. A group of mature women passed by and she laughed at the purple shirts they wore—Saddle up! Shut up! Hold on! She had to score one of those. And a cowgirl hat.

Roth held her near as they made their way through the crowded arena. The noise inside the place was thunderous, the lighting intense and the smell…interesting, but she loved it all.

Ooh, la, la, she thought when a group of cowboys

passed them, several tipping their hats at her. "I think you'd look good in one of those outfits, baby. What do you say we do some role-playing tonight?" When Roth didn't respond, she glanced up at him. "Roth?"

Roth's hard stare left the group who'd just passed them and settled on her. "You like that, huh?"

Something was off with him. He lacked the warmth that had been present just moments ago. What had changed? Then it dawned on her. *The group.* Had the men tipping their hats at her bothered him? As if Roth could read her thoughts, he smiled and nestled her closer against him.

Leaning in close to her ear, he said, "I'll show you a real cowboy when we get back to the room," then winked.

There was her naughty man. Still, what had prompted the shift she'd seen in him? He'd never displayed any hint of jealousy before. Not wanting to ruin the moment, she didn't address it. But she would when they returned to the hotel.

For the next two hours they occupied seats in the VIP section, directly above the chutes, and watched bull riding, tie-down roping, steer wrestling and undecorating. Tressa cooed during the mutton busting, where children raced sheep. Though it was quite entertaining, her nerves took a beating. Her worst fear was of one of them falling and breaking something. Luckily, it didn't happen.

After all of the main events had ended, they decided to do the vendor stroll. Hand in hand, they moved along the trails of vendors peddling everything from wallets to horse saddles. She joked about getting one of the saddles and strapping it onto Roth's back. He was all for it.

"So, what did you think?" Roth asked, draping his arm around her shoulders and pulling her close. "You think you want to add cowgirl to your résumé?"

"Heck, yeah," she said. "And tonight I'll show you how good I ride."

"Let's skip the vendor stroll and the Rawhide Steakhouse. We need to get back to the room right now."

Tressa bumped him playfully. "You are insatiable."

"I can't help it. You bring out the hungry beast in me. And the hungry beast has to pee. I'll be right back." Roth started away, but stopped. Backtracking, he pressed a hard kiss to her lips. "Don't move."

"I'll be right here."

Once Roth disappeared around the corner, Tressa leaned against the metal railing and watched the remainder of the kids' calf scramble. She laughed aloud as a dozen or more kids chased black calves. And she'd thought the mutton busting was amusing.

Tressa glanced up when something brushed her elbow. A tall, attractive, dark-skinned man wearing a black cowboy hat smiled down at her. Something happened in the arena and the entire place erupted in cheers and applause, drowning out whatever the man had said.

"What?" she yelled.

He leaned in uncomfortably close. "I said cowboys and cowgirls in the making."

"Looks that way."

Instead of him leaving, like she would have preferred, he continued chatting her up.

"You're not from around here," he said.

Curious, she asked, "Why do you say that?"

"There is close to a thousand people in this arena and you're the only one not wearing a cowboy hat."

Tressa sent a glance around her. He was right. She tossed her head back and laughed. "I am not. My *boyfriend* and I flew up today for the rodeo."

The man made a pained face, then placed his hand over his heart as if he'd been stabbed. "Oh, the *b*-word. You just killed me with seven letters."

"Nine, actually. But who's counting?"

Dead Man Walking continued to go on and on about something, but Tressa tuned him out. Then as if there had been a shift in the atmosphere, she glanced to see Roth standing several feet away.

Thank God. Maybe now this chatterbox would move on. But instead of Roth joining them, Roth's steel-cold gaze assessed Dead Man Walking, and judging by Roth's body language, *walking* was about to be dropped from the title.

Extreme turmoil clawed through Roth when he turned the corner to see some man bent over, whispering something in Tressa's ear. When she laughed, jealousy—a quadrillion times greater than anything he'd ever felt before—tore through him. His throat tightened and pain drummed in his temple.

What the hell had he said to her?

Roth shuddered, resisting the urge to charge like a bull and knock the bastard over the metal rails. He'd never been an insecure man, so he couldn't explain why the scene in front of him rubbed him so raw. But it did. His jaw tightened and every breath he took was drawn out and heavy, almost like fire in his lungs.

The cowboy kept yapping about something, but Tressa didn't seem to be paying a great deal of attention to him. Still, she hadn't sent him packing and that bothered him. Roth's hands tightened into fists when the cowboy stole a glance at Tressa's backside.

As if Tressa could sense his anguish, she turned toward him, the smile on her face melting into a frown. She shot him a worried glance, and he shot her a look right back—one of displeasure.

What in the hell was Tressa doing to him? He'd always prided himself on his ability to remain in control and be levelheaded, even during the direst of situations. Now here he was, acting like a rabid dog.

Composing himself, he held Tressa's probing gaze as he approached. The closer he got to her, the longer their eyes held, the less rage he felt.

"Hey, baby," she said, placing her hand on his back and ironing it up and down. "This is…"

"Frank," the man said, extending his hand to Roth.

Roth didn't really give a damn who he was, but he shook Frank's hand anyway, applying a hint more pressure than necessary. It'd been a warning—man code for *get the hell away from my woman*. One he was sure Frank got, because he pretended to see someone he knew, then hurried away.

Roth set his stone gaze on Tressa, but didn't speak.

"I think Frank's a zombie. He died when I told him I had a boyfriend, but he came right back to life," Tressa said and laughed. "He's awfully talkative for a zombie."

Roth knew she was trying to lighten the mood, but it didn't work. "Really? Well, at what point did you decide to tell him you had a boyfriend? When your head was cocked back in laughter or when he was whispering in your ear?" He instantly regretted his words and his pointed tone. What the hell was wrong with him?

Then it hit him. It hadn't been wholly about the cowboy. But the incident had triggered something already nagging him. It was seeing Cyrus's packed box still sitting in Tressa's closet when he'd gone to pick her up that morning. Why was she still holding on to the items? It was like she couldn't bear to rid herself of them.

Tressa's head jerked in what Roth took to be shock. Her jaw dropped and she stared at him as if he'd grown a second head. Recovering, she said, "I'll meet you at the car," and then stalked off.

Dammit.

Back at their hotel room, Roth tossed the door key, wallet and car fob on the dresser. The drive back had given him plenty of time to cool off, not to mention Tressa's cold shoulder. In that time he realized he'd acted like a jackass. Now he needed to make things right.

Tressa stood in front of the dresser, removing her jewelry. When he walked up behind her and rested his hands on either side of her waist, she flinched. He kissed the back of her head. "I'm sorry."

Her tired eyes met his through the mirror. "Okay." She pushed his hands away and escaped to the bathroom, slamming the door behind her with so much force the abstract painting hanging over the bed rattled.

Roth trailed her as far as the bathroom door but didn't enter. He started to move away until he heard her sniffles. Scrubbing a hand over his head, he pinched his lids together tightly, hating himself for bringing her to tears. "Baby, please don't cry."

Tressa didn't respond.

Blowing out hard, he rested his hands on either side of the door frame. "I saw red when I saw you with Frank. When I saw the way he was looking at you, checking you out…I felt threatened. I've never been an insecure or jealous man, Tressa. *Never.*" He paused. "But when it comes to you… I don't know. I'm different." He refrained from adding Cyrus's box to the mix. He knew that would only make things worse.

Tressa sniffled several more times, and he thought his heart would explode from regret. All he wanted to do was burst into that room, pull her into his arms, kiss every tear away and make her forget he'd ever hurt her. Which, clearly, he had.

"I'm sorry, baby."

On a whim, he tried the door. Surprisingly, it was unlocked. When he stepped inside, Tressa was sitting on top of the closed toilet seat, dabbing at her eyes with a tissue. It ripped chunks from his heart. He guided her to stand, then wrapped her in his arms. "I'll never make you cry again."

Several tense minutes ticked by, her silence driving him insane. Why wouldn't she just say something to him? Anything. And as if the universe had heard his innermost desires, he got his wish.

"I can't—" Tressa's voice cracked, but she soon continued, "I can't be with you, Roth."

Roth's chest tightened and a sharp pain shot down his arm. He swore he was having a heart attack. Was Tressa ending things? He prayed he'd heard her incorrectly. Rearing back, his worried eyes searched hers.

Tressa continued, "Not if you can't handle me talking to other men. I'm surrounded by men. All day, every day. You need to decide right now, before this goes any further, whether or not you can handle that. I want to be with you, Roth. But I won't be in a relationship where I have to walk on eggshells."

At the thought of losing Tressa, fear filled every cell in Roth's body. He didn't know what to do, what to say. He'd just got her. There was no damn way he would lose her over this, over his own insecurities. He cradled her face between his hands. "I don't want to lose you. Tell me what I need to do."

"You need to trust me. Trust that what we have is real and that I'd never do anything to hurt you, Roth. I get you've experienced a lot of heartbreak and disappointment in your past and it has lessened your faith in people. I can't be one of those people. Not if this is going to work. For this to work, you have to believe in us. I'm *crazy* about you, Roth Lexington, but I didn't like the man I saw tonight." Her eyes clouded with tears. "He scared me."

Jesus. What had he done? "I would never harm you. *Never.* Please tell me you know that." Several seconds that felt like several eternities ticked by.

"I know," she finally said.

Roth snatched Tressa into his arms and held her like he'd never held her before. He greedily claimed her energy. It gave him strength. "Be patient with me, baby."

"I will." A second later she pulled away. "You won't always get to simply say *I'm sorry* and expect everything to be okay. *I'm sorry* won't always be enough."

He nodded his understanding. "Is it enough now?"

When she nodded, he pulled her back into his arms. He may have denied it before, but there was no way he could any longer. He was falling in love with this woman. And the thought of *ever* losing her scared the hell out of him.

Chapter 14

Tressa checked her watch again. The third time since she'd occupied one of the tables inside Tender Hearts Memorial Hospital's café. Cyrus had dodged this moment long enough. If he didn't show up this time, she would take his things to the incinerator and burn them. The junk had cluttered her storage closet and life long enough—two and a half months to be exact. She'd been dead serious when she'd given him an ultimatum: either meet her to collect it *today* or it would be ashes.

He'd chosen the former.

He was officially twenty minutes late. No call. No text. No nothing. *So typical.*

Was he calling her bluff?

Well, he had ten more minutes to show, or she was out of there. If he missed this opportunity, he wouldn't get another.

Choosing to meet in a public place had been a great idea. She was glad Vivian had suggested it. Vivian had also suggested bringing a Taser, but she didn't feel that was warranted. Cyrus wouldn't harm her. However, her mother used to say you just never knew what desperate folks were capable of, especially when pride and ego were involved.

Tressa scattered the troubling thoughts. *Ugh.* She just wanted to get this over and be done with Cyrus, so she could focus on better things. An image of Roth filled her head. Just the thought of that man calmed her. She couldn't wait to see him tonight. Just like with the rodeo trip a month ago, he was being just as tight-lipped about where he was taking her on their date.

She ran her fingers through her shockingly short hair, still unsure how she felt about the new cut or going natural. Change, she reminded herself. The fact that Roth had loved it brought a smile to her face.

A crackle of lightning was followed by a deep rumble of thunder that shook the building and caused her to jolt. When she glanced up, Cyrus was strolling through the café doors. Had the ferocious weather been announcing his arrival?

Cyrus's unhurried steps suggested he had no idea that he was already late. Tressa shook her head in disgust. Oh, he knew; he just didn't care how his actions would inconvenience her. It was amazing how much clearer you saw things once someone had deceived you.

Once he finally approached the table, Tressa skipped a customary greeting. "I don't have long."

"And hello to you, too, sweetheart. Yes, I'm well, and I hope you're the same. My day? Oh, it was lovely."

Tressa rolled her eyes at his smugness. Why in

the hell did he believe she'd offer him any type of cordialness?

"What the hell happened to your hair?"

Tempted to say her man liked it, she ignored the question instead. "Thank you for finally showing up." Cyrus unbuttoned the caramel-colored, ankle-length wool coat he wore and placed it on top of the box containing his belongings. Why in the hell was he getting so comfortable? After removing his hat and scarf, he placed them with the coat, then eased down into the chair opposite her.

Tressa motioned toward the box. "I believe that's everything. If anything is missing…" She shrugged.

His eyes leveled on her. "You don't care, right?"

"Right."

Cyrus clasped his hands in front of him and leaned forward. "Why are you being so damn difficult? I made a mistake. Aren't I entitled to one?" His tone was a mix of frustration and impatience. "You've always been so damn stubborn."

"Well, my stubbornness is no longer your problem now, is it?"

Those steel-gray eyes darkened. "You were supposed to be my wife and just like that you want to walk away. I was good to you. You never wanted for anything. I loved you, still love you," he said through gritted teeth. "Even despite the way you've treated me the past few months."

She stood, refusing to sing this same old song with him. "I truly wish you nothing but the best, Cyrus. Enjoy the rest of your afternoon."

Cyrus stood with such urgency, his chair fell over. The swiftness of his action took her by surprise. In a blink, he was in her face. She'd never been fearful of him until this moment. The hardened expression he wore unnerved her. Maybe she should have given the Taser suggestion a little more consideration.

Cyrus grabbed Tressa's wrist and positioned his mouth close to her ear. "Are you sleeping with *him*? Don't think I haven't driven by your place and seen his SUV parked in the driveway. In my damn spot."

Tressa's eyes widened. "Driven by my place? Are you stalking me?"

Cyrus ignored the question, his tone softening. "Baby, please. Just give me another chance. I swear I'll be the man you need. I'll do right by you this time."

"You had your only chance to do right by me. Now, let go of my arm, Cyrus, before I scream bloody murder."

Instead of loosening, his grip tightened and Tressa thought he'd snap her wrist.

"Is there a problem here, Nurse Washington?"

Tressa recognized the voice and blew a sigh of relief, thankful for the intervention. Cyrus loosened his grip, and she yanked her arm away. Facing Dr. Benjamin Pointer, one of the cardiothoracic surgeons at the hospital, she said, "No, Dr. Pointer, everything is fine."

Dr. Pointer slid his gaze to Cyrus. If she had to translate Dr. Pointer's expression, it stated: *though I might be Ivy League–educated, I'm from the streets.* Obviously, Cyrus was good at nonverbal communication, because he backed away, collected his things and left with no further complications. But she had a feeling this wasn't over.

Several hours later Tressa and Roth were led to one of the many tables inside Tegria's, the Brazilian steak house she'd heard only great things about.

Roth pulled out her chair, and she eased down onto the burgundy leather. The aromas wafting around the room made her stomach growl. The fact she hadn't eaten since one that afternoon—seven hours ago—didn't help.

"This place is gorgeous," she said, scrutinizing the lengths of burgundy fabric draped from the high ceilings, the modern decor and the eclectic light fixtures.

"You're gorgeous," Roth said, taking her hand.

Though the lighting in the restaurant was dim, Tressa feared he would see the nasty bruise Cyrus's tight grip had left behind. Icing the area had done little to reduce the bruising. The chunky bracelet masked the black and blue for now, but she couldn't hide it forever.

Maybe she could say it was from a disgruntled patient. It was plausible. She'd been socked in the jaw once. No, she wasn't going to lie. Their relationship couldn't be plagued with lies. She had to tell him about her encounter with Cyrus. *No secrets*, she told herself. But not tonight. Tonight she just wanted to enjoy a beautiful evening with her man. Her trifling ex had ruined her afternoon; she refused to allow him to ruin her evening, too.

Tressa reclaimed her hand. "Mr. Lexington, are you trying to seduce me in this restaurant full of people, then entice me to join you in the restroom?"

"Don't give me any ideas, woman."

When he winked at her, a few naughty thoughts ran through her mind.

Roth dragged a finger along her forearm. "How was your day?"

"Long."

Concern spread across his face. "Did something happen?"

Tressa waved off the words. "No. Nothing out of the ordinary. Everyday stuff. A normal day in the ER. I just need a long, hot soak." To stop her babbling, she lifted her water glass to her lips.

He leaned in close. "I think I can manage a long, hot bath. A nice rubdown afterward. How does that sound?"

"Excellent. I'd like that a lot."

Over the next couple of hours Tressa and Roth enjoyed mouthwatering appetizers, several varieties of fire-roasted meats and sampled countless side dishes. To say she was stuffed would be a gross understatement.

"So, Chef Washington, does Tegria's get your seal of approval?"

"Absolutely. I am officially in love with this place."

"Did you save room for dessert?"

"Are you kidding me? If I eat one more thing, I'll explode. Are you getting dessert?"

He nodded like an overly anxious child who'd just been offered free rein in a candy shop.

Tressa laughed. "Where do you put it all?"

"I have plenty of space left. I didn't eat as much as you did."

Tressa swatted him playfully. "I can't believe you just said that."

Roth snagged her hand and brought it to his lips. "You know I'm only playing with you." He kissed the back of her hand, then her palm. When he slid her bracelet to kiss her wrist, he went still. He squinted as if he didn't believe what his own eyes were seeing. Fine lines crawled across his forehead.

"What happened to your wrist? How'd you get this nasty bruise?"

Tressa's heartbeat increased slightly. This was not where and how she wanted to tell him. "Today…um… Today, I…um…" She cleared her throat. "One of my patients… He was high on meth and had a psychotic break. He thought I was an alien coming to abduct him." *So much for the truth. It was just one lie for the greater good*, she tried to convince herself. Still, she felt awful and guilty.

Roth's features hardened. "How in the hell did they allow that bastard to manhandle you like this?"

Tressa glanced around to see if Roth's words had drawn any attention. Luckily, the place buzzed with so much chatter, she doubted anyone even gave them a sideways glance. "Roth, sweetie, calm down. It's really not that serious."

He made a sound similar to what a tortured animal would make. "Not that… It is that serious, Tressa. I don't like the idea of anyone putting their hands on you, especially aggressively enough to leave a mark like this."

To ease the mood, she said, "You know, I bet if you kiss it, you'd make it all better." She flashed a warm smile.

"Tressa, this is no joking matter. I—"

"Please." She batted her eyes for effect.

Roth studied her long and hard, his displeased expression finally softening. A beat later he peppered her wrist with delicate kisses.

"See, it's better already."

Roth flashed a lazy smile, then slouched back against his chair. She'd seen the fury that had danced in his eyes. Thank God she hadn't told him what had really happened. There was no telling what he would have done.

Continuing to give credibility to her story, she said, "I'm an ER nurse, Roth. I deal with the unpredictable day in and day out. Sometimes—" she lifted her arm "—things like this happen."

His tone sounded weary when he spoke. "Yeah, well, I don't like them happening to you."

In that moment Tressa had never felt so protected in her life. She kind of liked it. Too bad it was based on a lie. The greater good, she reminded herself.

Chapter 15

On the drive to his place, Roth wanted to be elated that he was getting quality time with Tressa, but what she'd revealed at the restaurant had dampened his mood and he just couldn't snap out of this funk. If he could just have five minutes with the asshole who'd done that to her wrist, he'd pulverize him.

Another wave of anger crashed through him. Sliding a glance in Tressa's direction elevated some of his rage. He squeezed her hand. "Hey." When she looked at him, he lost himself in the delicate expression on her face. How could anyone want to hurt her? "Have I told you how beautiful you look in that little black dress?"

"Only a hundred times, but a hundred and one couldn't hurt."

"You look beautiful."

"Thank you. And you are looking dapper yourself. I love that sweater on you."

"This old thing?"

A smile curled her lips before she turned away and slid her gaze back into the darkness outside the window. Something was bothering her. He could tell by the fact that she'd seemed distracted ever since they'd left the restaurant. But what? Then it hit him. The way he'd blown up when he saw her wrist. Had he scared her? *Damn.*

"Hey?"

"Hmm?"

This time Tressa didn't bother looking in his direction. "At the restaurant… I apologize if I overacted. If I frightened you."

Tressa turned toward him, a look of confusion on her face. "Frightened me? You didn't frighten me. You actually made me feel shielded. And I'm grateful that you have my back."

Roth brought her injured wrist to his lips. "I do. Don't ever forget that."

To his credit—and fault—he was a natural protector. If you messed with someone he loved, you messed with him. That had been the case with his foster brothers, waging war on anyone who'd done them dirty. Now it was the case with Tressa. And there was no limit to what he would do for her.

A short time later he pulled into his garage and shifted into Park. Hopping out, he moved around the vehicle to open Tressa's door. The fact he would fall asleep and wake with her in his arms lightened his mood considerably. Before he allowed her to escape from the vehicle, he leaned in and gave her a soul-shaking kiss, tasting and savoring every inch of her mouth. The sweetness from the mint she popped into her mouth right after leaving the restaurant still lingered and he tried his damnedest to rid her mouth of all its flavor.

When he finally pulled away, his lips ached. Damn, he had to have her. His erection made that painfully clear. Instead of a look of desire on Tressa's face, she donned one of concern. Enough was enough. He wanted to know what the hell was going on with her and he wanted to know now. Obviously, she'd witnessed that on his face.

"Roth, I need to—"

His cell phone vibrated, causing Tressa to pause. "I'll send it to voice mail."

"No, take it. It could be important. We'll talk inside."

Nothing was more important than she was, but it was late for anyone to be calling. He fished the device from the holder on his side. *Alonso.* A smile crept across his face. He and Vivian had been trying to get pregnant. Was Alonso calling to tell him he was going to be a godfather?

If so, that would mean Roth was about to be out of 50K. Years ago they'd agreed that whoever had a kid first, the other would establish a college fund. It'd started out as a joke because at the time, neither of them could have put their hands on that kind of money. But they knew one day they would be able to.

"What's up?" Roth greeted him, pushing open the door from the garage for Tressa to walk through. She mouthed that she'd be in the living room and he nodded with the promise to be there in a second.

"Shit, man. Vivian just got home from the hospital

and told me what happened today. That shit is foul. Is Tressa okay? Are you okay? I know you blew a gasket."

Roth figured Alonso was talking about Tressa's incident with the meth head. His jaw clenched at the ugly visual that filtered into his thoughts, some big, burly biker type slinging her around the room by the wrist. 'Course if he was a meth head, he couldn't have been so big, right? Still, that didn't pacify him. Roth opened the refrigerator door for a bottle of water. "Yeah, everything is good."

"It's a good thing Tressa didn't marry that lowlife. Any man who puts his hands on a woman is a punk."

Roth stilled and his brow furrowed. His jaw clenched tight enough to crush his teeth. He slid a glance to Tressa, who was walking around the pool table using her hand instead of a cue to sink balls in. Had her ex done this to her?

"Let me call you back, Lo."

"Okay, man. Peace."

Peace? Peace wasn't exactly something he was feeling at the moment. Taming his mounting outrage, he joined Tressa alongside the pool table. "Tell me what really happened to your wrist, Tressa." He kept his tone as steady as possible. "The truth this time."

Tressa tensed but relaxed a moment later, refusing to look at him. "Obviously, you already know the truth, Roth."

"Why did I have to hear it from someone else? You looked me directly in my eyes and lied to me."

Whipping toward him, she said, "What would you have done if I'd told you Cyrus did this, Roth?" She lifted her arm.

"Don't you mean what I'm *going* to do to his ass?

Right now, in fact." He turned to move away, but Tressa snagged the hem of his sweater, then moved around to block his path.

"Baby, he's not worth it."

"Why?"

"Because he's irrelevant."

Roth already knew that, but Cyrus's irrelevance wasn't what he was inquiring about. "Why did he grab you?" Tressa's eyes lowered, which told him what he'd suspected. "He knows about us?"

"He has an idea," she said, barely audible.

"And that's why this happened?"

When she didn't respond, he had his answer. He made a fist so tight his knuckles cracked. He was the one the bastard should have come for, not Tressa. But Roth would make sure he felt every ounce of that mistake.

Tressa rested her hands on his chest and he flinched.

"What are you going to do, Roth?"

He flashed her a do-you-really-want-to-know look.

Her words were sharp when she said, "You're not a monster, Roth."

His words were equally as pointed and urgent when he said, "No, I'm not. But I am a man who loves a woman and will be damned if I let—"

"Wh-what did you just say?" Tressa interrupted.

It took him a second or two to realize what he'd allowed to slip. *Shit!* This was not how he imagined saying those three words to her for the first time. He massaged his forehead. When he spoke, his tone was much calmer than it had been moments before. "I said—"

"You said you love me."

He scrubbed a hand over his head, handling her

trifling ex no longer seeming so urgent now. A lazy chuckle floated from him. "I guess I did."

"Did you mean it?"

She seemed almost hesitant to ask.

"Yeah, I did."

"I love you, too."

Roth crushed his mouth to hers and kissed her long and hard. Without breaking their connection, he hoisted her into his arms and climbed onto the pool table. "Do you have any idea how much I want you right now? I want you so bad I'm bordering delirium."

"Well, I can't have the man I love going insane. I guess that means you better take me."

Roth rolled her onto her stomach, then slowly unzipped the sexy-ass dress he'd fantasized peeling her out of all night. Leaning forward, he peppered tender kisses over her vanilla-scented skin. She always smelled so damn delicious. Maybe that was why anytime they were together he wanted to eat…her.

"You're always so gentle," she whispered.

Kissing his way to her ear, he said, "Not tonight, baby. Not tonight."

"I think I like the sound of that."

Roth made his way down her body, pushing her dress to her hips and exposing the black lace panties she wore. Her butt cheeks peeked from under the material. The sight was arousing as hell.

Dipping forward, he placed a kiss to her lower back. Tressa shivered, then moaned a low hum of delight. The sound made him all the more eager to please her. "You like that, I see."

"I like it anytime you touch me."

A confident smile spread across his face as he slid

her panties down her legs and over the sparkly black stilettos she wore. Those stayed on. Starting at her lower back, he dragged an unhurried finger across the dip, along the split of her buttocks and to her core.

Tressa squirmed when he teased her with a bent finger, gliding his knuckle up and down her clit. She moved her hips in sync with the movement of his finger.

"Faster, Roth."

Instead of doing what she requested, he stopped.

"*Nooo.* What are you—"

She drew in a sharp breath when he slid his thumb inside her canal and moved it in and out of her. Slowly at first, then faster. Tressa rode his finger, her ass bouncing in his face. He smacked one cheek, then the other, causing her to purr.

"You're so damn wet I could swim inside you," he said.

"I…I told you I like your touch."

"Oh, I'm going to be doing a lot of touching, teasing, tasting. I might drown tonight."

"I'll give you mouth-to-mouth."

Shit. He couldn't take this. Yanking his finger out of her, he climbed off the table and brought Tressa with him. "Let's get rid of this," he said, pulling the dress over her head and slinging it off to the side. Taking a step back, he admired her gorgeous body and thought about the sinful things he was about to do to it. His tongue glided across his bottom lip.

Tressa smirked. "You like what you see?"

"*Love* what I see." He motioned with his head. "Come here." Tressa glided toward him like a runway model. When they stood toe-to-toe, he said, "Kiss me."

She wrapped her arms around his neck and pulled

his mouth to hers. Their tongues fought a passionate battle. He walked her back until her body was pinned against the pool table. Lifting her, he placed her on the edge. Breaking their kiss, he said, "Lean back, but not all the way."

Once Tressa had propped herself up, Roth dipped forward and kissed her collarbone, then dragged his tongue down the column of her neck. Working his way down her torso, he sucked one of her hardened nipples through the lacy fabric of her bra.

"Roth, please."

"Please, what?"

"Make love to me. Make love to me now. Please."

Hearing her beg for him made him throb even harder. Whether she knew it or not, he was inflicting as much glorious torture on himself as he was on her. "Soon, baby. I promise." The reassurance was for them both.

Removing her bra, Roth pushed her ample breasts together and pulled both nipples into his mouth at once. He urged Tressa back, until her entire body was stretched out on the pool table. "Bend your knees." She did. "Now, spread yourself open for me."

Instead of her hand going directly between her legs, she put on a show for him. She started from her shoulders and slowly glided her finger down, teasing her own nipples along the way. He massaged himself through his pants, a primal sound rumbling in his chest.

Her hands continued their descent. When she spread her glistening lips, she dipped the tip of her finger inside herself, pulled it out and circled her wet index finger around her bead.

Roth intervened. "No. That's all mine."

"But I want you to watch me come."

"I want to make you come."

With that, he leaned forward, hooked his arms under her thighs and pulled her heat to him. Tressa's cries tore through the room the second his mouth touched her. He twirled his tongue around her clit, savoring the divine taste of her essence. Tressa held his head in place with her hands and ground against him.

"Roth..."

Her labored breathing told him she was close to exploding. When he suckled her clit, she fell apart. She slapped her hands against the table, her nails dragging across the fabric. Her back arched and her body bucked. He didn't pull away until Tressa's body had relaxed. In a flash, he was out of his clothes and into a condom. Joining Tressa, he rested her legs on his shoulders, leaned forward and drove inside her.

"Yes!" she cried out over and over again.

Roth delivered powerful thrusts, one after the other. Tressa screamed, cried, stuttered his name. Her nails dug into the backs of his arms, but the pain didn't hinder his performance. Hell, she could have ripped out a chunk of his flesh and he wouldn't have stopped, couldn't have stopped. Her wetness, her warmth, held him captive.

"I love you," he said. Why he'd said it at this particular time, he didn't know. But it felt like it needed to be said at that moment. Tressa tried to say something, but he crushed his mouth to hers. His words were the last ones he wanted her to hear before she plunged into ecstasy.

A beat later Tressa pulsed around him as an orgasm claimed her. Her cries were captured by his mouth.

Her body shook under him. The more she pulsated, the closer he came to his own release.

There wasn't an image on the face of the earth that could keep him from tipping over the edge. He wanted this too badly. But he tried to stave off the impending release, imagining shit like a cuddly koala bear nibbling on a leaf, a giraffe urging its calf on wobbly legs, even an orange-and-white-spotted koi fish eating its meal.

Nothing helped.

The orgasm slammed into him like an out-of-control semitruck. He roared like a lion declaring war on a territory invader. Pumping until he couldn't muster another damn stroke, he collapsed down next to Tressa and pulled her into his shaky arms.

Once his breathing calmed, and he regained the ability to speak, he said, "I need you to trust me, Tressa. And I need to be able to trust you. This can't work if either of those major components aren't in place."

Tressa came up onto her elbow and eyed him quizzically. He answered before the question escaped.

"You lied straight to my face, baby. I get why you thought you had to, but I need honesty, Tressa. I've been lied to my entire life. I need the woman I love to love me enough to always be truthful with me, no matter how much it might hurt. I need that."

Tressa slowly nodded. "And I'll give that to you."

It would be one of the best gifts he'd ever been given.

Chapter 16

Tressa lounged on the white leather sofa in the VIP section of The Underground. The place hadn't changed since the last time she'd been there. She remembered several months back and cringed. Though the night of her engagement party had ended in disaster, something much more beautiful had emerged.

Her gaze sought Roth on the stage. Damn, he was sexy as hell when he played that sax. Obviously, she wasn't the only one who thought so. Every woman in the place seemed drawn to the mesmerizing sound of his instrument, but Tressa noted one in particular.

Her eyes narrowed on the exotic-looking beauty in the very revealing emerald green cocktail dress. All night the woman had seemed more captivated with Roth personally than his playing abilities.

She'd never been the jealous type, but a ping of resentment prickled her skin. Dismissing the woman as simply an adoring fan, she trained her gaze on Roth again. A rush of heated desire coursed through her. Damn, she couldn't wait to get him naked. She bit at the corner of her lip. The black fedora could stay.

As if he'd sensed her undressing him with her eyes, he glanced in her direction. Their gazes met and held. Something sparked in his eyes that needed no translation. Longing. Clearly, she wasn't the only one with sinful things on her mind. The man had turned her into a sex piranha. She nibbled on him any chance she got.

Roth ambled down the stage stairs and cut his way through the sea of two- and four-top tables until he stood directly in front of her. He serenaded her and, boy, did he do his thing.

Every note that escaped from his saxophone danced through the air and crash-landed directly in her heart. Just as if it were his touch, she could feel the passion in his music. A brilliant smile touched her lips. By his actions, he'd told the entire room one thing…she was his. The enormous gesture filled her with pride.

When Roth finished his soulful melody, he took her hand, guided her to her feet and pressed a gentle kiss to her lips. The entire place erupted in applause.

The band continued to play, drawing the crowd's attention away from them.

"That was beautiful, baby." A tear she could no longer contain escaped her eye. Roth swiped his thumb across her cheek, causing her skin to tingle.

"Don't cry," he said.

"Sorry. Beautiful things make me do that."

"Huh. I've never seen you cry when you look in the

mirror." He kissed her again. "I'll join you shortly. I love you."

Tressa smoothed a hand along his cheek. "I know."

"How?"

"You just played me a love song."

He smirked, then started away.

"And I love you, too," she said.

"Forever." He winked and continued toward the stage, accepting handshakes and compliments.

"Forever," she mumbled to herself.

Tressa escaped to the bathroom to check her makeup. *Not too bad,* she thought, removing the tube of ruby-red lipstick from her clutch to freshen her lips. A toilet flushed behind her and she jerked. She'd assumed she was there alone. A young woman walked out. Gayle, if she remembered the woman's name correctly. She'd been the hostess at the entrance when they'd arrived.

"Hey," the woman said, pumping several squirts of soap into her palm.

"Hello. Gayle, right?"

The woman nodded. "Oh, my God, Roth's performance was amazing. You must feel like a queen."

Actually, she did feel quite regal. "He's a talented musician. And yes, I do feel majestic."

Gayle dried her hands. "Girl, if I had a man who serenaded me, I'd probably have twenty kids."

They shared a laugh.

Tressa and Roth wouldn't be making any babies tonight, but they would definitely be performing some baby-making actions.

"I know India hates the day she let that one slip away. Even if she was too dumb to recognize what she had, as she put it."

The words snagged Tressa's complete attention. *India? Who in the hell was...* "India?"

"India Breemer. She owns The Underground," Gayle said as if Tressa should have known this. "I'm surprised the two of you haven't met."

Not as surprised as she was by these revelations.

Gayle shrugged. "Well, she has been traveling a bit lately." She checked her watch. "Uh-oh. I better get back on the floor before India notices I've been gone more than five minutes." Gayle laughed. "She may look all gentle in that green dress, but she's a queen cobra in disguise."

Tressa forced a bye as Gayle exited the room.

Green dress? A knot looped and tightened in her stomach. The woman who'd taken so much interest in them—*him*, she corrected—was Roth's ex. Why hadn't he mentioned any of this to her? Why hadn't he told her he played at the exact same club owned by his ex? *His ex.* An ex who *clearly* still had a thing for him. He'd had plenty of opportunities, including on the drive here.

She shook her head, never recalling Roth ever uttering India's name. Her first instinct was to stalk out of that bathroom, stroll right up to India, stick her hand out and introduce herself. "Hi, I'm Tressa Washington, Roth's girlfriend." Then stick her tongue out for good measure.

Tressa laughed at her own childishness. There was no need to go that route. Heck, after Roth's performance, Tressa was sure everyone in attendance knew she and Roth were more than just friends. That put her a bit at ease.

Still, why hadn't he told her? This kind of information should have come from him, especially when he was all about being completely honest. She scrutinized the red-and-black era-specific decor inside the posh room. *This damn club.* She shook her head. *This damned club is a curse.*

Roth stored his saxophone in the case, then snapped it shut. Now that his set was over, he could concentrate all of his focus and attention on his sexy muse. He stirred below the waist when he summoned an image of Tressa in that off-the-shoulder wine-colored dress. Yeah, he planned to drink her up tonight.

Judging by the expression on her face when he'd played for her, she'd loved every second of his attention. He loved seeing her smile, especially if he was the one putting the smile on her face.

"Now I guess I know why I never received the text containing directions to your cabin."

Shit. He turned to see India standing behind him. The form-fitting, low-cut dress she wore should have done something to him, but it didn't. Yeah, Tressa had ruined him. And he was okay with that.

Roth's spontaneous decision to invite India to his cabin had been a result of desperation. That night—the night of Tressa's engagement party—he'd needed something to take his mind off the fact that Tressa would never be his. He recalled his foolish words to India. *If I text you the address to my cabin, would you show up?* Her answer had been a sultry, "I'll be waiting." Inwardly, he chastised himself for having been so damn brainless.

"She's beautiful," India said. "Is it serious?"

He nodded. "Yeah, it is."

India's face lit into a bright smile. "Congratulations."

She draped her arms around his neck. "I'm happy for you."

When her glittered lips pressed against the side of his neck, he snatched away and held her at arm's length. "No."

India smirked. "I'm just making sure." She winked and sashayed from the room.

Grabbing up a hand towel, Roth scrubbed at the side of his neck, making sure there was no remnant of India's lipstick remaining. Satisfied with the results, he left the room to join Tressa. As irrelevant as it was, he should probably mention his past with India. He hadn't before because the past was the past, right? But now, he didn't want to feel as if he were keeping anything from Tressa.

Before Roth could escape from the back, Gayle stopped him in the hallway.

Gayle bit at the corner of her lip as if she dreaded whatever she needed to say. "I may have got you in hot water. I'm sorry."

His brows bunched. "Hot water with whom?"

"Tressa," she said hesitantly. "I was chatting with her in the bathroom and may have mentioned India." She rested her hands on either side of her face. "I'm sorry, Roth. It never dawned on me that she didn't know about the two of you."

"Thank you for letting me know, Gayle."

She apologized again, then hurried off.

Roth could read Tressa well enough to know what she'd learned about him and India bothered her, because this was not the jovial woman he'd walked away from several minutes ago. Easing down beside her on the leather sofa, he captured her hand and kissed the inside of her wrist. "What's wrong?" he asked, fishing to see if she'd tell him about her conversation with Gayle.

"Nothing."

"Dance with me, beautiful."

"Roth, I don't really feel—"

"Please." He kissed her wrist several more times. "Pretty please."

Tressa sighed. "One song."

If she was only giving him one song, he'd better make it a good one. On the way to the dance floor, he whispered to Ernest—one of the guys on stage. The man gave him a nod.

"What did you say to him?" Tressa asked.

Enveloping her in his arms, he flashed a half smile. "I told him I needed a special song for a very special woman. I dedicate this song to you."

A moment later the band performed John Coltrane and Johnny Hartman's "My One and Only Love."

They swayed to the soothing melody. When Ernest's regal baritone voice poured through the room, Tressa relaxed in his arms. Roth had to give it to Ernest; he could melt ice when he crooned. The man could sing his ass off, really sing. Not any of this new age stuff you could barely decipher from shrieking.

Roth and Tressa never broke eye contact.

While he'd been lost in her dancing brown eyes plenty of times before, this time was different. He was swimming in her soul and experiencing all the effects of being there. Giving her the opportunity to come clean with him, he said, "You want to tell me what's going on?"

"Maybe you should tell me, Roth. I know about you and India. What I don't know is why I had to hear it from someone else. It feels like you're trying to hide something."

"Tressa…" he said coolly, "India and I happened a long time ago. I'm not trying to hide anything from you. I honestly didn't think my past—which is exactly what it is, the past—with her was all that relevant. Any interaction we have is *strictly, strictly*," he repeated, "business." Except for the part where he'd invited her to his cabin in a moment of despair. But he had sense enough to keep that to himself.

"Is the fact that she's still in love with you irrelevant, as well?"

Roth threw his head back in a laugh. "Baby, now you're being ridiculous. India and I haven't been a couple in, what, five years."

"Is she the one who hurt you?"

He eyed her but didn't respond.

"I thought so. I've seen the way she looks at you, Roth. You may be blind to the fact, but she still has a thing for you. I'm a woman. I know the signs, and hers is a flashing big-ass green neon light."

"And I have a thing for you," he said, hoping to deviate from this topic. If India still *had a thing for him*, he didn't care. Nor was it any of his business. Tressa was his business. The only person's feelings he could control was his own. And all his feelings were wrapped up in Tressa. "Do the signs show you how much I love you?" He nuzzled her neck. "What color is that big-ass neon sign?"

Still stone-faced, Tressa rolled her eyes at him.

Placing a finger under her chin, he turned her head back to him. "Do you trust me, baby?"

"Yes, but I don't trust her."

"And you don't have to. Your trust should be with me, not her." He captured her hand and placed it over his beating heart. "Do you feel that, woman?" he asked, his expression serious.

"Yes," she said, some of the bite gone from her tone.

"Every beat belongs to you and you alone, Tressa Washington. Every woman in this building could strip naked right now and throw themselves at me, and I would throw them all back. Why? Because I'm not going to do shit to jeopardize what we have. You're the best thing that has *ever* happened to me, woman. The very best thing."

Tressa blinked rapidly, but it didn't keep the tears from falling. For the second time that night, he swiped a thumb across her cheeks.

"You keep messing up my makeup."

"If it all ran down your face, you'd still be the most beautiful woman in here."

"Flirt," she said with a lazy smile.

"Are we okay? Really okay?"

Tressa studied him for a moment, then nodded. "We're really okay."

He tilted her head back and kissed her tenderly. "Good."

Chapter 17

Tressa sat alone at one of the two tables inside the nurses' lounge, forking at the now-wilted lettuce in the bowl in front of her. Pushing the grilled-chicken salad away, she cursed the thoughts that tortured her. Two weeks had passed since she'd learned about Roth and India's past, and it'd been all she could think about—*obsess over*, she corrected.

Though she'd told Roth his continuing to play at The Underground didn't bother her, it did. It bothered her a lot. When in the hell had she become so damn insecure? The answer came quickly—when her ex's mistress crashed their engagement party, and at the same club owned by Roth's ex.

A thousand times she'd reminded herself that Roth was absolutely nothing like Cyrus, and she believed it. Still, she couldn't stop thinking, *What if?* Yes, she trusted Roth, but this had nothing to do with trust and everything to do with the idea of history repeating itself. Tressa recalled the things Roth had said to her that night in the club and smiled, the memory lightening her heavy thoughts. Roth was a good man. She had nothing to worry about.

Tressa hadn't asked for any details about his and India's history—and he hadn't offered any—but she remembered their conversation from the cabin. They hadn't been right for each other and she'd cheated on him. He'd never mentioned they'd remained friends.

Then it hit her.

Could her true issue be the fact that Roth hadn't offered to stop playing at The Underground? She wouldn't have let him, but shouldn't he have at least offered?

The door swung open, and Vivian sauntered in. "I am not going to miss these crazy hours," she said, dropping into the chair opposite Tressa.

Vivian had decided to resign from her position at Tender Hearts Memorial Hospital to focus more of her time on the project her husband, Alonso, was developing downtown geared at helping the homeless and disenfranchised. She was going to miss working with her best friend, but Tressa truly understood and supported Vivian's decision.

Vivian's eyes slid to the discarded salad, then slid to Tressa. "Everything okay? You usually don't let food go to waste."

They laughed.

Sobering, Tressa said, "Should I feel some kind of way about Roth not offering to quit playing at The Underground?"

"I don't—"

"He didn't even say, 'I'll find another club to play at, because I know it bothers you that India is my ex.'" Saying it aloud, Tressa accepted how selfish she sounded, but wasn't she making a genuine point?

"Why do—"

"I mean, he didn't even take my feelings into consideration by not offering to leave. But really, why should he? He's been playing there far longer than we've been dating. Why should he alter his life for me?"

"It really—"

"But isn't that what people do for love? Make sacrifices?" *Ugh.* She buried her face in her hands. "What is wrong with me? I've never been this weak."

"Take a breath, Tress. You're not weak, you're in love, ladybug."

Tressa didn't dispute Vivian's words.

"You should talk to Roth. He'll respect your concerns. That man loves the hell out of you."

A slow smile curled Tressa's lips. "I've never loved any man the way I love Roth. It's like this beautiful, pleasurable, terrifying plane ride. At times I desperately want to plant my feet on the ground. But at others, I love how he makes me feel like I'm flying, soaring so high in the clouds I feel like I'm in heaven. The way I love him scares me, Vi. I can feel him in my soul. He's brought so much joy, so much happiness into my life. I can see myself spending the rest of my life with him."

"I wish you could see your face right now. You are glowing." Vivian narrowed her eyes at her. "Are you pregnant?"

Tressa tossed a balled-up napkin at her. "No." However, the idea of her stomach swelled with Roth's child—his children, as many as he wanted—wasn't a bad one.

"You're afraid because of what happened with Cyrus, but you can't let fear dictate your steps. I believe you told me something similar once." Vivian smiled, then continued, "I read something once that said sometimes the greatest love of your life comes after the biggest mistake of your life. Would you agree Cyrus was the biggest mistake of your life?"

"Oh, yeah. Without a doubt."

"Then that means Roth is the greatest love of your life." Vivian took Tressa's hand. "I've noticed such an amazing change in you, Tress. Every single day you walk through that door confident and sure. I hadn't seen you that way in a long while. Trust me, I know loving someone with everything inside you is daunting as hell, but do it anyway. It's so worth it."

Tressa released a heavy sigh, allowing her worries to escape with the warm air. Vivian was right. Love— this kind of love—was worth it.

Roth and Alonso sat at the round conference table inside Alonso's office, neither uttering a word. Roth drummed his fingers over the polished wood as if he was playing his sax, even humming a melody in his head. John Coltrane and Johnny Hartman's "My One and Only Love." So fitting. Alonso spoke, pulling him from his thoughts of what he'd done.

"Tell me again what happened."

A sly grin spread across Alonso's face, then he laughed. Well, who could blame him? The story was so damn bizarre, it was hilarious. One minute he'd been sitting behind his own desk, in his own office, the next... His gaze fell back to the shiny black ring box placed in the middle of the table. "I went inside the jewelry store to purchase Tressa a cross necklace—"

"And you came out with a mammoth-size rock."

Alonso laughed and so did he. "Man, I swear to God that ring called my name. The next thing I know..." He pointed to the five-carat emerald-cut diamond ring. "I'm walking out with that and without a single regret in the world."

"Well, I for one had no doubt you were going to make Tressa your wife. The two of you are meant for each other. I don't think I've ever seen you happier than when you are with her. You know I support this 100 percent. I'm happy for you, man."

Alonso stood and Roth followed suit. After exchanging a brotherly hug, they both dropped back into their seats.

"So when are you going to pop the question?"

Roth ran his hand over his head. "I was going to do it tonight, but decided to wait until this weekend. I want it to be special, something memorable. She deserves that."

"Are you doing it at the club?"

"Hell, no," Roth said. "Tressa would say no for sure. She's convinced that place is a jinx." And could anyone blame her? But he was about to leave her with at least one good thought of the place. "You guys should come out for the show on Saturday. It'll be my last."

Alonso's head jerked back in what Roth took to be surprise. "What? You're leaving The Underground?"

Yeah, he couldn't believe it either, but it was time. "Tressa says she's okay with me being there, but I can tell it bothers her. And honestly, if the shoe was on the other foot, I might be a little leery about her working so closely with her ex, too. I know she trusts me, but I don't want to give her any reason to worry." The fact that India had started acting oddly after seeing him and Tressa at the club had been another reason, but he didn't mention that one. After Saturday, it would no longer be an issue.

"Are you going to play elsewhere?" Alonso asked.

He'd contemplated it but decided he'd much rather spend his free time with Tressa. "Nah. I'm going to chill for a while."

"Speaking of exes. Whatever happened with that situation with Tressa's?"

Roth shrugged. "Strangest thing. He left her a voice mail message apologizing profusely for manhandling her at the hospital, then said he was moving out of state and that he wished her the best."

Alonso barked a laugh. "Did you have anything to do with his decision to flee the state?"

Roth sat back in his chair and crossed an ankle over his leg. "Come on, man. Tressa forbade me to confront that slimy bastard."

"Uh-huh. What did you do?"

Alonso knew him too damn well. "I may have contacted him to say I would ruin his career and his life, if he ever contacted Tressa again."

Alonso gave a knowing smirk.

And they left it at that.

Alonso fell back against his chair and intertwined his fingers behind his head. "We've come a long way, man. We got lucky. I think about all the shit we've been through..." His words trailed off. "We're two blessed brothers. Good—scratch that—*great* women. Love.

Happiness. Success. We did it. Just like you always said we would."

Yep, he had said it, over and over again. Believing life had far more to offer was what had got him this far. He couldn't agree with Alonso more; they were blessed and happy and in love with great women. And soon, he would ask his muse, his lover, his heartbeat, to be his wife.

Yeah, life was good. He eyed the ring box. And it would only get better.

Chapter 18

By the time Saturday rolled around, Roth's nerves were shot, so much so he'd walked out of the damn house and forgotten Juliette—his tenor sax. The one thing he hadn't left behind, the black ring box. In less than two hours, he planned to lower to one knee and ask Tressa to spend the rest of her life with him.

A tiny voice whispered, *Will she say yes?*

Confident, Roth answered with a swelled chest. Of course she was going to say yes. Why wouldn't she? If he wasn't sure of anything else, he was sure Tressa loved him. A second later he frowned. But what if…

Roth shook the negative thoughts away, but somehow they fluttered right back. Her last engagement hadn't exactly gone off without a hitch. What if she'd decided marriage wasn't for her? What if he proposed and she said no? What then?

Arriving at The Underground, Roth pulled into a space in the back lot. The same space he'd occupied the night he'd discovered Tressa in the back of his SUV. The night that had patterned his feet on this glorious journey toward love. This had to be a good sign, right?

Of course it was.

So why did he have that nagging feeling?

Roth considered calling Tressa to make sure she hadn't got held up at work or, worse, changed her mind about meeting him there. This wasn't exactly her favorite place. Just to see the look of surprise on her beautiful face, he needed her there to hear his announcement that tonight would be his last performance.

If she didn't show, it would definitely put a hitch in his arrangements. He'd have to scrap the plan to propose on a carriage ride through downtown. It didn't matter where he proposed. All he knew was he had to do it tonight. He couldn't wait another moment.

As if he'd sent some kind of vibration across town to Tender Hearts Memorial Hospital, his phone rang, Tressa's name flashing across the screen. Actually, the words *My Queen* scrolled across the screen, because that was what she was to him, his queen. "Hey, beautiful."

"Hey, handsome. I only have a second."

Alarmed, Roth said, "I hope you're not calling to stand me up, because that would really suck." *Really suck*, he repeated to himself.

"No, but I may be late. Thirty minutes, an hour tops. I'm sorry." Her words dripped with regret.

"Is everything okay?"

"Yes, just a madhouse here. Full moon. I gotta go.

Love you to pieces and I'll make my tardiness up to you in countless sinful ways."

"I'm definitely going to hold you to that. Love you, too." And tonight she'd know just how much.

Tressa had some hell of apologizing to do. Her one hour, *tops*, had stretched into two. And of course she'd missed Roth's performance. Inside, she squinted and scanned the room for him, but he was nowhere in sight. He was there because his SUV was still parked out back. Plus, he wouldn't have left without calling to tell her. If there was one thing her man was, it was considerate.

A swamped Gayle, the hostess she'd met her last visit there, pointed her toward the back of the building. "Try the back. I saw him walk that way earlier," she said, then bustled away. "Oh," she called back, "tell him I said I'm really going to miss our old-school R & B chats."

"Going to miss—" Gayle was off before Tressa could finish her thought. Was Gayle leaving The Underground? Probably so. She'd got the impression the woman didn't care very much for India.

India.

Just the thought of her name grated Tressa's nerves. Pushing the raw feeling aside, she headed in the direction she'd been pointed.

The sconces affixed to the beige walls provided minimal lighting along the hallway. Fortunately, Tressa didn't need any illumination to locate Roth; she simply followed the boom of his elevated tone. And he sounded pissed.

Approaching the partially opened door, she reached

for the handle, but froze when she heard a woman's voice.

"You are full of shit, Roth."

Her tone was just as heated as Roth's had been.

"I don't owe you shit, India."

India? Tressa's eyes narrowed as if she was trying to see through the door. What in the hell were they arguing about? A lover's quarrel came to mind, but she debunked the term.

"But why, Roth? Why now? Was it the kiss?"

The air vacated from Tressa's lungs. Had they kissed? Her heartbeat kicked up a notch or two and her breathing grew ragged. She wanted to burst through the door right then, but her need to hear more was greater.

"When I was in jeopardy of losing this place, it was your performances that saved it. We built this place together, Roth. We're a team. Now what? You're going to walk out on me? Just like that? No notice, no explanation, no nothing? Just some tonight-will-be-my-last-performance bullshit announcement you made to the entire club without having the decency to let me know first."

Tressa rested a hand on her trembling stomach. Roth was leaving The Underground? India's tone softened to a pitch that could be considered seductive, and rage shot through Tressa. Still, she held a level head.

"We're good together, Roth. You know we are."

For whatever they'd shared to be in the past, Roth and India sounded mighty cozy. Tressa's cheek burned with outrage with the possibility that she'd been played for a fool. Again. Now she really wanted to explode into the room, but her heavy feet were rooted to the tile floor, making her unable to crash their party or flee the building. The urge to do both overwhelmed her.

"I'm sorry, India."

Roth's tone sounded sympathetic, as if in some way he regretted what he was doing.

India continued, "You can't leave."

Roth's tone sounded exhausted when he said, "What do you want from me, India? What the hell do you want from me?"

"Everything. I love you. I never stopped loving you, Roth. After all these years. I want you to admit you still have feelings for me, too."

Tressa's stomach knotted as she waited for a response from Roth. Did his silence mean he still loved India or that he didn't feel the question warranted a response?

When he finally spoke, his tone lacked sentiment. "I don't love you and haven't for a long time. We had our chance. It just wasn't meant for us."

When India spoke again, her tone was crammed full of emotion, and Tressa was almost certain she was crying.

"Then why in the hell did you invite me to spend the weekend with you at your cabin a few months ago? Was it just about sex?" she spat.

Tressa's brows furrowed. *Invited her to his cabin?* India had been the woman… Her chest grew heavy and bile burned the back of her throat.

A beat or two of silence lingered before Roth said, "Yes, it was."

"You liar. Do you think I don't see how you look at me when I walk past? Do you think I don't know what ran through your mind when I undressed in front of you earlier?" Her tone grew soft again. "You wanted me then, Roth, and I know you want me now."

Instead of Roth refuting the claim, he said, "Goodbye, India. Have a great life."

The door flung open with so much force, Tressa flinched. Her lips parted, but nothing would escape. She dragged a hand across her cheek.

"Tressa?" Roth's hard expression melted to one of shock.

Sure of the questions racing through his mind, she said, "I heard everything. I—" The words snagged in her throat. "I have to go. I..."

She closed her eyes briefly to subdue the queasiness she was feeling. When Roth touched her, she shoved his hand away. Forcing her feet to move, she took several clumsy steps back until she bumped into the wall, then made haste down the corridor.

As she fled, Tressa felt like she was in one of those fun houses at a carnival. Everything ran together into a hazy blob of shapes and colors. Her head spun, forcing her to stop and rest her hand against the wall to regain her equilibrium.

"Baby—"

Standing behind her, Roth rested his hands on her waist, preventing her from getting away. She lacked the energy needed to push him away. "You lied to me, Roth. Everything was a lie," she said more to herself than to him. "You told me there was nothing between the two of you, that I could trust you with my heart, that I would never regret falling in love with you." Tears clouded her eyes. "You lied, because I regret it plenty."

"Please don't say that, Tressa. Please." He kissed the

back of her head several times. "I never lied to you. I swear, there's nothing—"

Needing to look into his eyes, she turned toward him. "Did you invite her to your cabin for sex?"

"Just listen, baby, please. I—"

"Did you invite her to your cabin for sex, Roth?" Tressa spewed the words like venom.

Defeat danced in Roth's eyes. "Yes."

"Then there's something."

Tressa's gaze slid past Roth and leveled on India propped against the door frame, watching them like her favorite sitcom. For a brief second Tressa considered barreling down the hall to knock that condescending smirk right off her face. But what would be the point?

"Can we talk?" Roth said.

Drawing her attention back to him, Tressa refocused on the visibly exhausted man in front of her, the man she loved, the man who'd changed, rocked and shattered her world. "No."

Chapter 19

Instead of immediately leaving the community center where he taught saxophone lessons to disadvantaged kids, Roth stood with his arms folded across his chest, staring out the fogged-up window. The darkness outside mirrored his soul. A single ray of light hadn't penetrated through him since... He refused to even give life to what had happened several days ago at The Underground.

By giving Tressa her space, he hoped she'd realize how ridiculous she was being. Yes, what she'd heard was bad, really bad; he'd be the first to admit that, but she'd refused to even give him the opportunity to explain. She'd simply jumped to conclusions.

Waiting for her to come to her senses, he'd gone through a myriad of emotions. Today he'd welcomed anger. *How in the hell could she believe I'd ever do any-*

thing to hurt her? Roth sighed heavily. Watching that woman walk away from him had been like watching an alligator gnaw off your leg and not doing anything to stop it because you had no idea what to do.

Dammit, you should have done something.

"Mr. L?"

"Yes!" *Damn.* Roth massaged his temple, took a deep breath, then turned toward a stunned-faced Sebastian, one of the kids in his class. "I didn't mean to snap at you, Sebastian. I apologize."

Sebastian ambled toward him, his hands tucked inside his tattered jean pockets. The ten-year-old was as timid as an abused puppy, but Roth saw something in the kid. Maybe a little of himself at that age. Roth had quickly outgrown his timid stage. Maybe Sebastian would, too.

"What's up, man?"

Sebastian lowered his head, lifted it, then lowered it again. "I wanted to make sure you were okay." He dug the tip of his worn tennis shoe into the scuffed industrial tile, his gaze never meeting Roth's. "You always tell us to practice, practice, practice at the end of each class, but you didn't say that tonight. You say it after every class. And before dismissing us, you always make us say, 'We're strong black men, and we matter.' You didn't do that, either."

Roth chuckled. *Damn.* He guessed he had been a little off tonight. Sebastian paid attention to everything, so it didn't surprise him that the inquisitive boy had picked up on his turmoil.

"So, is everything okay?" Sebastian asked. "You're not leaving us, are you?" He finally glanced up, pushing his wire-framed glasses up his nose.

The kid reminded Roth of a young philosopher. With the right guidance, he would do great things. Adjusting his mood, Roth said, "Dude, no, I'm not leaving you guys. You know how much I love teaching you knuckle-heads how to play. Even though I think the only reason most of you come is for the pizza on Thursdays."

Sebastian lowered his head, but Roth could see the smile that played on his lips. Every young man who participated in Roth's twelve-week-long academies were required to sign a pledge to take their lessons seriously. While each Tuesday and Thursday they showed up faithfully, he suspected the reward was what kept most of them so dedicated.

But he didn't care what it took to get them through the door. If they were in class with him, they weren't out in the streets causing or getting into trouble.

Then there were the two or three he had like Sebastian, who truly enjoyed learning to read music and play the saxophone. Their eagerness alone made this all worth it.

Roth placed a hand on Sebastian's shoulder and jostled him playfully. "I apologize for straying away from routine. I'll have it together by Thursday. I promise. Thank you for keeping me on my toes, man. I owe you."

"My dad stopped doing things he used to do right before he left me and my mom." Sebastian shrugged a scrawny shoulder. "I don't want you to leave, Mr. L. You're a great teacher and you don't treat us like kids. Plus, you buy us pizza." He smiled, revealing a missing bottom tooth.

"Don't worry. I'm not going anywhere," Roth said.

Sebastian's words hit home. If nothing else, Roth

understood abandonment. He would never do that to his boys. Or someone he loved.

For the past week Tressa had hidden her pain behind forced smiles and work. Still, no matter how brilliantly she smiled or how many hours she strolled the halls of Tender Hearts Memorial Hospital, Roth eventually invaded her thoughts. And when that happened, her heart shattered all over again.

Vivian grabbed another mozzarella stick off the table and crunched into it, drawing Tressa's attention. Tressa smiled at her best friend opposite her on the couch, who'd arrived at her place an hour ago with an overnight bag and comfort food: mozzarella sticks, chicken wings, pizza, garlic knots, fried ravioli and vanilla ice cream to wash it all down.

"You do know I'm trying to lose a couple of pounds, not gain," Tressa said, reaching for another one of the meat-filled ravioli and popping it into her mouth. She'd start fresh tomorrow.

Vivian grabbed another piece of pizza. "Tonight, calories don't count."

They shared a laugh.

Tressa appreciated what her friend was doing, but it wasn't necessary. "You don't have to babysit me, Vi. You're a married woman. You should be home with your husband."

"I want to be here. Alonso won't be home till late. He's supposed to be meeting Ro—" Vivian stopped abruptly.

"You can say his name. I won't go ballistic." Though she might just burst out crying. It truly could go either way.

To think a few weeks ago she'd been the happiest woman alive. Now look at her, wrapped in a blanket on her couch stuffing her face with food. *Pitiful.* Happiness was clearly reserved for individuals who didn't let the likes of love get in their way. *Love.* She growled at the low-down, trifling emotion that had brought her far too much pain.

"You know what's funny, Vi? I really thought this was it. I really thought I'd get my happy-ever-after. I thought Roth was the one." Her voice cracked with unintended emotion.

"Roth *is* the one."

Did Vivian not recall all the things she'd told her, all the things she'd overheard that night, backstage at the club? How could she still believe in Roth? Tressa blew out a heavy sigh, choosing not to address Vivian's words. "I'm done."

Vivian eyed her quizzically. "Done with what?"

"Love, men, relationships. I'm done with it all. Obviously, this is a sign I'm meant to be alone."

Vivian barked a humorless laugh. "You don't mean that, Tress."

Yes, she did. "I trusted him, Vi. I trusted every kiss, every touch, every intimate moment I shared with him. I trusted him." She shook her head. "I should have known better. I know the games men are capable of playing. I just never thought Roth—" She stopped at the onset of emotions she felt. No way would she cry. *No. Damn. Way.* Her head tilted back against the cushion. "I'm done."

"I can't believe what I'm hearing. From *you*, of all people. You are the freaking ambassador for all things love."

"Maybe once. Not anymore."

Vivian sat up ramrod straight. "When I foolishly wanted to run from Alonso, it was you who gave me a swift kick in the ass and brought me to my senses."

"And I'm happy for what you and Alonso have, Vi, but I'm beginning to think love is just not meant for me."

"So you're just going to give up?"

Tressa folded her arms like a defiant child. "Yes."

"The Tressa *I* know wouldn't just bow down and take it. She would fight for what she loved, *who* she loved. And trust me, I *know* you love Roth just as much as he loves you. And another thing, you may be *done with love*—" she made air quotes "—but love is not done with you."

Tressa eyed her best friend. Why in the hell was Vivian so distraught? She was the one going through the perils of love.

Tressa ached to stress just how wrong she thought Vivian was. But since Vivian was clearly the new poster child for love, Tressa kept her comments to herself. And just for the record, she wasn't giving up; she was giving in. Love had taken her through too damn much.

No, she didn't care what anyone said. She was done with love.

Chapter 20

Roth had thrown himself into his work—arriving at the office at the crack of dawn, not leaving until pitch dark. Why? Because designing a new aircraft was the only thing that kept him half-sane and his mind off Tressa. That and playing the sax, but somehow, playing always brought his thoughts back to her.

When his cell phone rang, he tossed a glance at the clock. *Eight. Shit.* He was late. Taking the call from Alonso, he said, "I lost track of time. I'm on the way."

Alonso rattled off something about it being packed and he'd go ahead and grab a table. Ending the call, Roth logged off his computer before midnight for the first time in days, gathered his belongings and headed out to meet Alonso—who would undoubtedly spend the evening trying to cheer him up. Why? Because that was what best friends did for each other.

A half hour later Roth sat inside the Flaming Arrow Bar and Grille, nursing a glass of top-shelf bourbon. Conversation swirled around him, people happy and celebrating life. He envied them, because at this moment his life was shit. Without Tressa, his…life…was…shit. He was man enough to admit that.

So why in the hell hadn't he done anything about it?

Scanning the room, his eyes lingered on blissful couples hugged up in booths, whispering sweet nothings to each other. He saw people on their way to being happy couples, offering enduring gestures in hopes of solidifying their positions in each other's lives. Then there were the individuals obviously searching for that love connection, exchanging interested glances and warm smiles. Lastly, the handful clearly looking for just an evening with no commitment.

Him, in a past life.

Roth grumbled and damned everyone around him for carrying on with their lives while his life was falling apart around him. What had love done to him? And why had he allowed Alonso to talk him into coming here against this backdrop of happiness?

Alonso claimed another one of the habanero wings from the platter. "Have you called her?"

After giving her some time to come to her senses—which hadn't happened—he'd decided to help her along by reaching out. She'd shunned him like a leper. "A hundred times. I feel like a stalker." He took a swig from his glass. "She hasn't blocked me yet. I guess that's a good sign."

"She will come around," Alonso said.

Roth wasn't so sure about his friend's optimism. The anger he'd suppressed came back with a vengeance.

"Why in the hell am I sitting around, moping? I haven't done anything. I never touched India. If Tressa can't trust me, then maybe…" His heart wouldn't allow him to complete the sentence.

"Tressa loves you, Ro. She's just hurting. Give her time to sort all her feelings. She will come around."

"Yeah, well, I'm hurting, too. She tossed me away, man. She tossed me away just like every other—" Stopping abruptly, he finished the contents of his glass and motioned to the waitress for a refill. Enough of this feeling-sorry-for-himself bull. "I'm good. How do I even know it's worth it anyway?"

Alonso pushed his plate away and wiped his hands. "What if Tressa walked in with another man right now?"

Alonso's words ignited an inferno inside Roth, and lava flowed through his veins. His jaw clenched so tightly he thought the bones would shatter. The mere suggestion of another man getting any of Tressa's time caused him to see red.

Alonso jabbed a finger at him. "That reaction, my friend, is how you know it's worth it."

Roth's brow furrowed.

Alonso barked a single laugh. "You looked like you were ready to kill over a woman who hasn't spoken to you in over a week. That's love, man. And love is always worth it."

Roth's heart rate slowly decreased. He massaged the tension from the back of his neck. "Could you have thought of another way to make your point?"

Alonso flashed his palms. "Hey, I did what I had to do. You were there for me when I had given up any hope of getting Vivian back. You had my back. Now it's time for me to repay the favor."

Alonso clapped Roth on the shoulder. Roth couldn't be mad at his best friend for getting his blood boiling. That's what true friends did. They said and did whatever they needed to do to keep each other from making devastating mistakes.

"Thank you, man," Roth said.

"My pleasure. Now, let's strategize on how you're going to get your woman back."

There was no need. Roth knew exactly what he needed to do.

Tressa rolled her head to the side to glance at the clock sitting on her nightstand. Four o'clock. In two hours she had to be up, bright eyed and bushy tailed. Unfortunately, she wouldn't be either. She'd be surprised if she'd got four full days' worth of sleep total in the past two weeks. One thing was for sure; she couldn't keep going like this.

Her eyes landed on the black tourmaline on the nightstand, and she thought about Roth. He hadn't had a nightmare since she'd given him the crystals. She'd attributed it to the tourmaline; he'd attributed it to her. Recalling how grateful he'd been by her gesture warmed her, along with words he'd said. *Woman, you're the answer to my unspoken prayers.* The amount of compassion that had glowed in his eyes...

Tressa swallowed down the building emotions. She hated to admit it, but she missed Roth like hell. The way he touched her—as if she were a rare stone. The way he kissed her—with so much intensity it left her breathless. The way he made love to her—as if he was giving her chunks of his soul.

Tressa pinched her eyes together to fend off her tears. Her head suggested she needed to get over Roth, but her heart gave other advice; sound advice, she chose to believe. So why was she lying there in bed alone and not beside the man she loved?

Because you are a stubborn fool, Tressa Washington. And it has cost you the best thing that's ever happened to you. A beat later, tears rolled from her eyes.

She cried.

She cried long.

She cried hard.

She cried ugly.

She cried for the pain she'd denied feeling over her loss.

She cried for the many times she'd rejected how much she missed Roth.

She cried for the countless moments she'd told herself she no longer loved him.

She cried for…for the mere fact there had been no laughter in her soul since she'd walked away from him.

She cried until there were no more tears left.

Had losing Roth truly been a sign she deserved to be alone? She certainly believed in signs, especially ones she'd asked for. But she hadn't asked for this. She would have never asked for her heart to be ripped from her chest. She would have never asked for this type of pain.

But had she?

She'd been the one who'd refused him the opportunity to explain. She'd been the one who'd walked away, her hurt overshadowing the guidance of her heart. She'd been the one who'd, for the past few weeks, refused to reach out to him. Had she asked for this?

Two hours later the alarm sounded and Tressa slammed her hand onto the snooze button. She draped her arm over her eyes, cursing the light penetrating her blinds.

It can't be six already.

Dragging herself from the bed, she charged through her morning bathroom routine, then headed for the kitchen to consume a trough of coffee. The fragrant java smell greeted her the second she opened her bedroom door. *Thank God for coffee machines with timers.* The first sip of the strong brew caused a twitch in her lips that would have normally blossomed into a smile.

Today she didn't feel like smiling. Would she ever again? Feel like it or do it?

Leaning against the counter, she steadied the cup between her hands. She just couldn't continue like this. Her job performance was taking a hit and so was her health. Over the past two weeks she'd experienced elevated blood pressure and heart palpitations. She blamed it on sleep deprivation and stress. Her eyes lowered to her mug. Of course, her increased caffeine intake could be a contributor, as well.

Relinquishing the mug, she grabbed her insulated tumbler and filled it to the brim. Checking the time, she grabbed her purse and headed for the door. If she was late again, Ms. Kasetta, the toughest charge nurse in the South, would have her head—and her job, no doubt.

Stopping abruptly, she cursed, veered back to the kitchen and lifted her keys from the hook. "Can't go anywhere without these." Satisfied she hadn't forgotten anything else—like her brain—she hurried out the door.

The second she stepped foot on the porch, Tressa gasped and dropped the tumbler. The top popped off and hot coffee ran everywhere. The mess only fazed her for a millisecond, sending her gaze back to her lawn.

Stunned by the display, her eyes swept her front yard. "What the…" Countless airplanes littered her grass. Stepping over the spilled coffee, she descended the stairs. Her purse slid from her arm and *thunked* to the ground. There was only one person who could have accomplished this. Roth.

Her eyes brushed from one side of the yard to the other. Where was he? Was he still there? Watching her, maybe?

Collecting one of the lavender planes, she unfolded it. Sure enough, a message was scribbled inside, just as she suspected. "Memories are priceless. One of the best ones I have is making snow angels with you." A smile touched her lips. It was one of her best, too.

She lifted another lavender plane. It, too, contained a memory message. "We don't remember days, we remember moments. I'll never forget the exact moment I fell in love with you." Tressa flipped it over, expecting more to be written. Disappointed that there wasn't.

She wanted to know when.

She swallowed hard and blinked back tears. Choosing a white airplane this time, she pulled it apart as if gold coins waited inside for her. This one was a Maya Angelou quote.

"'People will forget—'" Her voice cracked and she recited the rest in her head. The last line, *people will never forget how you made them feel*, was written in all caps. Roth's penned words followed. *You make me feel invincible.*

Tressa clapped her hand over her mouth, a single tear sliding from her eye. *Oh, my God. Oh, my God.*

A red plane caught her eye. Scanning, she realized it was the only red plane there. Moving to the center of the yard to collect it, she took a deep breath before unfolding it. *I promise* was the only thing written. Tressa brows bunched. *I promise?* What did he promise?

Before she got the opportunity to ponder the cryptic message any further, a paper plane soared overhead and landed a foot or two in front of her. She turned urgently, expecting to see Roth standing there. Nothing. Where in the heck was he?

"Roth?"

Her eyes scanned the yard again, even kneeling to look under her vehicle. Bemused, she gave up her search for him and collected the steel blue plane. She gasped, recognition setting in immediately. This was *her* plane, the one she'd crafted at the cabin. She studied her hand-written words—smeared, but somewhat still legible—on the warped piece.

"How—"

"When I first read your words, *he makes me feel like I'm soaring*, I swore I'd do any and everything in my power to always make you feel that way."

The soothing sound of Roth's steady tone caressed her like tiny fingers exploring every inch of her body. Gathering her thoughts, she turned to face him. The sight of him sent a *boom* through her system, reviving every part of her that felt as if it'd died since they'd been apart. For the first time in what she labeled forever, she felt alive again.

Her eyes took in every inch of him. His handsome face, his thick shoulders, the brown short-sleeved shirt he wore, the jeans that hung perfectly from his toned frame, even his all-black tennis shoes. *I've missed you*, she said, but only in her head.

Lifting the plane, she said, "How did you get this?"

"Glen."

Her eyes widened. "It made it to town."

Roth chuckled that beautiful sound she'd missed so much.

"Almost. He came across it when he was searching for his dog who'd run off into the woods. And since I'm the only one known for crafting paper planes, he put two and two together."

Dumb luck or fate. She wasn't sure which, and she didn't care. All that mattered was that it'd brought Roth back to her.

Roth cupped his hands in front of him. "I have something to say. Just listen. Please."

Tressa nodded.

"Baby—" He paused as if he'd suddenly recognized an error he'd made. When he started again, he dropped *baby*. "*Tressa*, I get it. It's not always about what happened. Sometimes it's about perception, appearance. The things you heard… I get it. They were awful and they hurt you. But there are two important things I need for you to know, then I'll leave."

Leave? The word rattled her.

"First, I have never, ever been unfaithful to you. The things you heard…" He shook his head. "I never did anything that would disrespect you. I put that on my life."

"What about the kiss—" The idea of Roth kissing another woman froze the words in her throat.

"She kissed me on the neck. It wasn't provoked, nor

wanted. That's the only time in five years her lips have ever touched me."

So much passion radiated from Roth's words that all she wanted to do was drape her arms around him. But she resisted. "You said you had two things to tell me."

"The second thing… I love you more than life itself. You are my life. I'll never stop fighting for you, for us. Because that's what I do, baby. I fight for what I love, for who I love. I'll never stop fighting. That's my promise to you."

Tressa swallowed hard, her chest aching with emotion. Roth reached up to touch her but abandoned the thought.

"That's all," he said, his voice cracking. "I won't take up any more of your time." He backed away, then turned to leave.

"When—" She took a deep breath, then started again. "When did you know?"

Roth turned slowly. Asking for no reference, no clarification that they were even talking about the same thing, he closed the distance between them. "When you took my hand at the cabin and placed it over your heart. My heartbeat fell in sync with yours at that very moment. And I knew I would love you for the rest of my life. These past two weeks—" he lowered his head as if to hide shame "—let's just say my heartbeat has been irregular."

Tressa thought about her own suffering. She'd contributed her palpitations to sleep deprivation, stress and caffeine. But could it have been from Roth's absence? Could their hearts truly beat in such harmony?

Obviously.

"I owe you an apology, Roth. I was closed-minded

and judgmental. I never gave you the benefit of the
doubt or the respect you deserved. I let fear guide me.
But that's no excuse for how I treated you. I'm sorry.
I'm so sorry. And I would do anything, *anything*, to
have you back in my life again." Tressa's heart pounded
against her rib cage and tears rolled down her cheek. "I
don't deserve a second chance, Roth, and I'm not sure
I deserve you, but I want—I *need*—you." She took a
deep breath, then continued, "You are that spark that
ignites everything good in me. I should have been the
one fighting, Roth. I should have been the one fighting
for you, for us. I'm fighting now."

This time when Roth reached out to touch her, he
didn't pull back and neither did she. When the pads of
his thumbs swiped across her skin, she closed her eyes,
feeling as if her entire spirit recharged from his touch.

Roth rested his forehead against hers. "I'm lost without you."

"I love you, Roth Lexington. I love you with every
cell in my body. Do you forgive me for hurting you?
Can you—"

His mouth crashed against hers, the feel of his lips
causing a surge through her entire body. They'd kissed
plenty of times before, but this time was unlike anything
she'd ever experienced with him. She gladly accepted
every urgent swipe of her tongue, meeting his urgency
with eagerness of her own.

They kissed long, hard and for what felt like an eternity. Then reality kicked in. Tressa jerked away from
his addictive mouth. A look of pure desperation flashed
across Roth's face.

Tressa laughed for the first time in far too long.

"Work." She laughed again, this time at the ridiculous timing of her words.

Roth's brow furrowed. "What?"

"I have to get to work."

The pained expression slid from Roth's face. A second later he scooped her into his arms. "You're going to be a few minutes late."

"If I'm late again, I'm going to be in the unemployment line."

Roth carried her toward the house. "Then you can focus on opening your own culinary studio. Or be a stay-at-home mom."

Tressa's jaw fell open, but she couldn't find her words.

"Keys," he said, climbing the stairs.

Unscrambling her brain, she said, "Somewhere on the ground."

A minute later they pushed through the front door. Roth slammed the door shut and pinned her against it. Again, his mouth claimed hers, but only for a short time. With urgency, he snatched her shirt over her head, then her bra came off. Untying the strings of her scrub pants, he pushed them down over her hips. Pressing his body firmly against hers.

"You feel that?" he asked against her mouth.

"Yes. And I want it."

A sexy sound rumbled in his chest seconds before he snaked a hand down her panties. He massaged her slowly, gently. Intense moans rolled past her lips.

Roth kissed her gently on the lips. "Tell me you love me more than any other man walking the face of the earth and that you always will."

Did he really expect her to form a sentence? As

good as his hand felt between her legs, all she could do was moan.

"Say it, baby. Please. I need to hear it. I desperately need to hear it."

"I…" The tingling sensations of an orgasm stalled her words. "I love you…more than any…"

"Any other man," they said in unison.

"Walking the face of the earth, and I always… I always will. *Oh, God!*"

The orgasm nearly crippled her, shattering her into a thousand pieces of useless matter. Her knees buckled, and she fell against Roth's solid chest. Scooping her into his arms, he carried her to the bedroom, laying her partially on the bed, and finished removing her clothing. Dropping to his knees in front of her, he claimed her core with his mouth. It wasn't long before another powerful orgasm overtook her.

Like lightning, Roth rid himself of his clothing, blanketed her body with his and drove himself into her, hard and deep. Tressa cried out in pure ecstasy. He delivered wild, delicious strokes that fogged her brain. It felt good. It felt so good.

"Don't stop, Roth."

Roth pinned her legs back and drove into her even harder. "Woman, don't ever make me suffer without you again."

Jesus, it felt so good. "Okay."

Roth growled a primal sound, his body trembling. A beat later he throbbed inside her, sending her over the edge once again. Delivering four or five more lumbering strokes, he collapsed onto her. Their heaving chests rose and fell in tandem. Roth's sweat-silken forehead wet the crook of her neck and his labored breath tickled her skin.

"That was…amazing," she said.

Roth raised his head, eyeing her with admiration. "You're amazing. Are we good, baby? I mean, really good?"

Tressa smoothed a hand down the side of his face. "We're good. Really, really good."

Finally wrangling herself from Roth's arms, Tressa darted into the bathroom, took the fastest shower she'd ever taken, threw on her bra and panties and barreled from the room. "I'm so—"

She stopped so suddenly, she nearly toppled over. Her jaw dropped, staring at the bed. "Roth?" she said, scanning the room for him. Taking a few steps closer to the bed, she rested a trembling hand over her mouth, while the other pressed into her quivering stomach.

Tressa reached for the black box sitting in the center of the bed, withdrew as if it would bite her, then reached for it again. Popping the top, she gasped at the huge diamond ring inside. Her hands trembled so badly, she nearly dropped the box.

"I want to spend my life with you, Tressa Washington."

She turned to see a fully dressed Roth standing behind her. How did he keep sneaking up on her like that?

"I want to share with you my hopes, my dreams, my ups, my downs, my fails, my successes. I want to share it all with you."

Somehow, her brain formed a sentence. "You want to marry me?" She wasn't sure if it had been a comment or a question.

"Yes. I was supposed to do this the night we…" His words trailed off. "I've made plenty of mistakes in my life, Tressa. But the one thing I got right was falling in love with you."

Her eyes clouded with tears at his sweet words. Falling in love with him was something she'd got right, too.

Roth claimed the black box and removed the ring. "I know this is probably not the most ideal moment, but…" He lowered to one knee. "Tressa Nycole Washington, will you marry me? I'll make you happy, baby. I'll make you so happy."

Tressa half sobbed, half laughed. "I'm in my underwear, Roth. But yes! Yes, yes, yes, a hundred times. I'll marry you."

Roth slid the ring on her finger, stood, hoisted her into his arms and kissed the past few weeks without him away. Pulling back, he said, "You should probably call to let someone know you won't be in today and possibly tomorrow, either. We have lost moments to make up for."

"Forty-eight hours is an awful lot of time. What do you have in mind, Mr. Lexington?"

"Well, soon-to-be Mrs. Lexington—" he kissed the ring on her finger "—I plan to spend all of that time reminding you how it feels to soar."

Oh, she didn't need a reminder. "I remember. In fact, I'm soaring on love at this very moment." But she'd make the call anyway, because the idea of spending the next forty-eight hours, plus the rest of her life in his arms, was too damn tempting to pass up.

Epilogue

Tressa stared into Roth's concerned eyes, not recalling a time in the past couple of years she'd ever seen her husband so shaken. Though she was the one in the hospital bed, he seemed to be suffering far more.

Roth blotted the sweat from her forehead. "Breathe, baby. Just like we learned. You got this and I've got you. What you go through, I go through, remember?"

"Okay, trade places with me," she said through labored breaths.

One of the labor and delivery nurses chuckled.

"All right, Tressa, one big push and your bundle of joy should slide right into the world. Ready?" Dr. Fiona asked.

After nine hours of labor, hell, yes, she was ready. "Let's do this."

Several hours later Tressa watched Roth with their

son, Shiloh Randall Lexington. The way he admired the newborn brought tears to her eyes. Thinking back, she remembered how tears had run from Roth's eyes when she'd told him she was pregnant.

A week after their engagement, she and Roth had married at the only place she would consider—the cabin. At that time she hadn't believed her life could get any better. It had.

Maybe she should give partial credit to Nettie and the top secret family recipe she'd shared with Tressa as a wedding gift. "Because you're family now," Nettie had said.

Turned out, it wasn't a food recipe at all. It'd been a recipe for a happy marriage. It was an interesting tradition, and she planned to pass a copy down to her boys when the time was right and hoped they committed each ingredient to memory and prepared the dish every day, just as she had.

2 cups of romance.
2 cups of laughter.
2 cups of trust.
2 cups of respect.
2 cups of sharing.
2 cups of tenderness.
2 cups of courtesy.
2 cups of consideration.
2 cups of attention.
4 cups of patience.

She'd altered hers a tad, adding 16 cups of great sex.

"Knock, knock."

The door creaked open and a very pregnant Vivian

waddled through, holding Justen's hand—Tressa and Roth's three-year-old son. She never used the word *adopted*, because she felt just like she'd given birth to him. Justen's thick black curls bounced as his short legs carried him across the room to Tressa's bedside. He stood on his tiptoes to see her.

"Mommy, okay?" he asked in his tiny voice.

To be so young, the child always showed such empathy for others.

"Mommy is fine, my sweet boy." She brushed a finger over his caramel cheek. "Let me look at you. I think you've grown two inches. Do you want to meet your brother?"

Roth waved Justen over.

Justen patted Tressa's hand. "Justen be right back. 'Kay, Mommy? I'm a big brother now."

"Yes, you are, son." Tressa blinked back tears. God, she loved that little boy. What had started out as a temporary emergency foster placement had turned into a permanent adoption. She thanked God every day for bringing Justen into their lives.

"Congratulations, Mama," Vivian said, approaching the bed and taking Tressa's hand.

"Congratulations to you, Godmama. I hope Justen wasn't too much trouble. He has the energy of several Jack Russell terriers."

"He was good practice," Vivian said, rubbing her protruding belly. "Having him at home with us made me even more eager to meet these two handsome fellows."

"Where's Alonso?" Roth asked, finally pulling his attention away from his boys.

"Yeah, I can't believe he let you and those boys out of his sight for one second." Tressa laughed.

Vivian shook her head. "Well, the godfather of your children is passing out cigars and telling anyone who will listen that he has another godson. Pray for him."

The room filled with laughter.

Vivian washed her hands and claimed Shiloh. It was the funniest thing ever watching her use her stomach as leverage. While Vivian entertained both boys, Roth pulled a chair to Tressa's bedside.

"How do you feel, Mama?"

"Like I've hit the lottery, over and over again."

Roth captured her hand and kissed the inside of her wrist. She loved when he did that.

"Woman, do you have any idea how happy you make me, how much I love you and our sons, our family?" he asked in a hushed tone, his eyes full of emotion.

"I do. You show me every single second of the day." She ran a hand over his stubble. "Man, do you have any idea how happy you make me, how much I love you and our sons, our family, our life together?"

"Of course I do, but will you keep telling me every single day?"

"I'll do one better. I'll keep telling you until I take my very last breath, because you make me feel, Roth Lexington. You make me feel like I'm soaring on love."

* * * * *